RASHMI NARZARY is a dog lover at heart, an author by passion and an independent editor by profession. Awarded the Sahitya Akademi for Children's Literature in 2016 for her collection of short stories, *His Share of Sky*, creative storytelling and reimagination of folklore and legends are her forte. Literarily, socially and academically acclaimed, her debut novel, *BLOODSTONE, Legend of the Last Engraving*, is one such historical fiction woven around the legends of the Kamakhya Temple.

Her latest novel, *An Unfinished Search,* is a historical fiction portraying the rootlessness and loss of identity that war and partition of nations cause.

Narzary's work is being taught in universities and researched for doctoral thesis and has been translated into other Indian and foreign languages.

Her growing up years in Shillong, where she started her education in Pine Mount School, left an indelible, endearing mark on her bond with the hills and nature. Little wonder then that abundance of nature rules her otherwise simple, easy narrative style. Her driving passion for storytelling made her degree in Economics and post graduation in Human Resource Management take a backseat.

She lives in Guwahati with her husband, a former IAS officer, in a home that abounds with pets and large flocks of visiting birds.

*Whistles of the Siphoong* is Rashmi Narzary's seventh book.

# TALES FROM ASSAM'S BODO HEARTLAND

## WHISTLES OF THE SIPHOONG

RASHMI NARZARY

Om Books International

First published in 2024 by

**Om Books International**

**Corporate & Editorial Office**
A-12, Sector 64, Noida 201 301
Uttar Pradesh, India
Phone: +91 120 477 4100
Email: editorial@ombooks.com
Website: www.ombooksinternational.com

**Sales Office**
107, Ansari Road, Darya Ganj,
New Delhi 110 002, India
Phone: +91 11 4000 9000
Email: sales@ombooks.com
Website: www.ombooks.com



ISBN: 978-81-19750-24-5

Printed in India

10 9 8 7 6 5 4 3 2 1

To every talebearer
who has lovingly kept
lores, legends and the past
alive and moving,
through time and generations

# Contents

# PRELUDE

'Long ago, in the ancient times, long before the winds from these plains and hills of lush green forests and deep blue rivers blew far over the mountains and across the seas to let most conquerors and wanderers know about their existence…' so narrated Asidoh Buri, the talebearer. 'Know, Bodosa, it was then that your forefathers migrated in batches from the region between the headwaters of the Yang-Tse Kiang and the Hwang Ho rivers in the north west of China to arrive in this country between the second millennium BC and the first millennium AD. So, you, Bodosa, belong to the Mongoloid stock, to the Tibeto-Burman branch.'

'After they reached here,' she went on, 'they let themselves be absorbed into the societies of these fertile, stretched-out plains. These were the first Bodos, the earliest inhabitants of this enchanting land of Assam. They occupied an extensive part along the plains and valleys of the rivers Barak and the mighty "Burllungbuthur"—the Brahmaputra, as most call it. Their kingdom extended very far away to what is now no more ours, Bodosa—far away to Dimapur. That land, Dimapur, is now a part of what belongs to the Nagas. Nagaland, they call it. Even now, as in those ancient times, your brethren are scattered all over the north and along the foothills of Bathou's abode in the Himalayas. Yes, Bodosa, I speak of Nepal and Bhutan. A handful of Bodos have made their home in parts of the Garo Hills in neighbouring Meghalaya. They are in the west, too—in Bengal. And today, they are the largest group among all tribes in the plains of this unparalleled land of Assam. They speak the same Bodo language as you and I, wherever they are settled—a language that has its roots among the Sino-Tibetan faction. Of course,' she chuckled, 'there definitely might be little twists in how they make it sound. That is solely because of the influence of local languages over time. Even the Ramayana and the Mahabharata bear tales of valiant Bodo kings in these eastern parts of the country. From the times of the mythologies right down to the times of written and recorded history, many a powerful Bodo king had established and ruled under different dynasties before the whites came from the far west, across the seas. You belong, Bodosa, to a mighty and fearless race. Know that!'

Asidoh Buri was a living chronicle of the indigenous Bodos. She had nothing documented, yet everything was stowed in her unfaded memory in detail—from the knowledge of the amazing array of medicinal herbs and methods among the Bodos to the wars and battles they fought and won, and the borders they marked for their lands through the ages. She would sit near the Shiva temple at the peak of Baokhungri Hill to retell the tales of this great race that is steeped in folklore and mystique, which has innumerable legends surrounding it because of the lack of a recorded history. Asidoh Buri had all of these legends at the tips of her four fingers and two thumbs on each hand. That's how she got her name. Asi doh. In Bodo, asi means fingers and doh, the number six. Most thought she was divine because of the colour of her skin. It was so pale a peach that on a moonlit night, it looked almost white. And set against that peach, unstained white lashes marked out her small, light-brown eyes, which seemed like translucent pools of water made brown with mud from the hills. No one knew her age, but her hair and eyebrows had always been as white as the snow on Bathou Bwrai's abode.

'And so,' she narrated, 'they, your forefathers, settled down as a farming tribe. They reared fowl and pig, and fished in the rivers and ponds. To preserve meat and fish when it were in excess, they sometimes sun-dried them and sometimes smoked and fermented them in bamboo hollows. The Bodos believed only in Bathou. In those days, the Bodos worshipped no deity, no idol. Neither did they have any fixed place of worship. However, for a physical representation of the formless, omnipresent Bathou, they prayed in front of the Sijou plant. And they offered their veneration to their long-dead ancestors. But as the seasons passed by, taking the decades and the centuries with them, the influence of other faiths and beliefs led to the worship of Shiva; and somewhere along the years, they began to bring Bathou and Shiva together. In the present times, of course, Bodos worship most other Hindu deities as well. And not to forget those of your brethren, Bodosa, who believe in Jisu Kristo (Jesus Christ).

'Ah, yes, your forefathers have also handed down their skill and tradition of rearing mugalatha (silkworms) on the mulberry plant to spin out yarns using which they wove the golden, dream-like silk you call muga, an exquisite fabric, fit for royals. And they have also raised the endi emphou (worms) on the eri plant to spin yarns of endi. From these, they mostly wove shawls. Bodo women have since the times of yore been weavers like no other, Bodosa, so deft they were at their handlooms! They wove for themselves the brightly coloured dokhonas they wear; yellow being the dominant one among the other colours of red and green. These they wove with intricate designs—agor, as they call them—of the beautiful surroundings amidst which they lived. These designs and motifs recreated the hills, dales and rivers, the plants, birds and butterflies and the stars, sun and moon into the costume which they draped around themselves.'

She then paused to tighten the tuck of that same costume she wore now, the dokhona, above her breast. Like the Bodo women of those ancient times, Asidoh Buri never wore a blouse. And then she resumed.

'The joubidei that you brew, Bodosa … yes, that rice beer; that too has been handed down by your forefathers. But mark my words. The ways of brewing it have been passed down through word-of-mouth and not through the written word, on leaves or paper. And soon enough, the jou came to be an integral part of all our rituals and festivities. That's how we celebrate the spring festival of Bwisagu and the harvest festival of Magw Domasi. That's how we worship Bathou during the Kherai Puja. Yes, Bodosa, with offerings of the jou. And the Bodos have been singing such beautiful folk songs and rhymes since those times! Songs that tell tales of love and angst, of forests and of battles, of kings, demons and witches. And there are such inspiring aroz methai (hymns) and soothing, calming lullabies as well! Ah, yes! I should not forget to mention the songs our people sing during work in the fields and during weddings and ceremonies. There are ballads too. Someday I shall sing these to you.' If she had a good listener, Asidoh Buri sang and even explained to them the many songs, rhymes and lores surrounding children's games, rites of birth and death and stories of spirits. Modai, as the Bodos called them.

'And they, your forefathers, handed down the art of making their own musical instruments to play during those festivals and rituals, sometimes in accompaniment to the songs they sang. All of these instruments are unique, Bodosa, and yet among them, the siphoong (flute) holds the greatest significance. Legend has it that the simplest yet most captivating instrument, the siphoong, came to be when the Bodos worshipped Bathou and were in need of song and music to entice the deity into descending upon the doudini, the shaman. They believed that because there can be no life without air and because it is but air that the siphoong breathes and blows through, it is the wand of the heavens, the most significant of all musical instruments in existence. However, it is together with the kham and the jotha that the siphoong's powers multiply manifold during the rituals.

'And that's why the Bodos then fashioned the kham—the long drums—out of hard wood from old, majestic trees in the forests. These they hung horizontal to their bodies with a cloth belt looped around their neck. And then they beat with their bare hands the drum's round sides made of animal skin. Thereafter, they procured the jotha, the thin, round plates of metal. You know, Bodosa, "jo tha" means "to stay together". Hence, they are used in pairs and brought together to create rhythm.

'Of course, equally relevant to the Bodos are the serja and the jabkhring. Ah! Such touching melody the four strings of the serja create! But you have to caress them with a small bowstring made of a thin strip of bamboo and a bunch of hair from a horse's tail. Now, didn't I mention the jabkhring?' She paused and pondered before resuming: 'It is a crescent-shaped piece of wood with oval holes. Into these are pinned small metallic discs that make a clanging sound.

'But of all these and a few more, the ones that we Bodos hold most dear and sacred are the siphoong, kham and jotha. And even among these three, as I have already told you, it is the siphoong that breathes life into the Bodo soul.'

Asidoh Buri paused and closed her eyes, as if trying to make something rise from slumber in the deep recesses of her memory. She took a long breath, opened her eyes and then spoke once more.

'I was a mere child, Bodosa, and since then I have been seeing a dream—a dream about three men. All three of them were descendents of this valiant race, which is why I had to narrate to you the story of the great Bodos. For, without knowing who they were or where they came from, you wouldn't know the dream I recall. Nor would you relate to the tales of these three men of my dreams.

'Three great and faithful friends, none of them were whole without the other two—just like the siphoong, kham and jotha. Each of the men played one musical instrument. And yet, he who blew into the siphoong always appeared the most vividly in my dreams.

'The siphoong is the wand of the heavens and conjures the magic of music without really being a magic wand. Just so, this person who plays it is noble of heart and reveres Bathou just like Oja Bwrai, the priest, without really being a priest. In my dreams, therefore, I find myself calling him by a name that sounds similar to Oja Bwrai, though not really Oja.'

'What is that name, Asidoh Buri?' Bodosa asked.

'Ojhai!' she replied.

# Chapter 1

# BARTER OF THE SIPHOONG

'Life, Birkhang, is a barter!'

Ojhai drew his siphoong, the flute, gently to his lips like he would his lover's slender wrist, as he talked to Birkhang. Ojhai and his siphoong together created such soulful music that it made every spirit and human, bird and beast, plant and pebble, virtuous or vicious, fall under a spell when notes from his siphoong brushed past them, leaving them craving for more. The most obstinate of elements yielded to the charm of those notes. As Ojhai closed his eyes and played, the notes from his siphoong cascaded gently through the tranquil winter night, across freshly harvested fields of rice and mist-filmed ponds of catfish and snakehead. He played for a while and then pausing to look at it, said again, 'Life is a barter. Plant a bamboo and you get a flute in return. It's all give and take, you see.'

Birkhang nodded. He was waiting for the lapping flames to ebb. He had brought with him a couple of snakehead fish and as soon as the flames ceased to rise, he would place them on the glowing embers. For sixty winters or maybe more, Ojhai, Daimalu and Birkhang had spent their winter evenings thus, by the fire. One played his siphoong, another sang along and the third roasted fish. And sometimes sweet potato, yam and pieces of pork too. A barter among them but also a bonding experience. Ojhai's daughter-in-law would then get them home-brewed jou and the old men would sip it gleefully with the fish after mashing it with crushed green chillies, salt and sometimes, if times were good, a wee bit of chopped onion.

Ojhai had known nothing and no one dearer to him other than his siphoong. It melted the heart to see him craft his siphoongs; such fatherly care he doled into making them! He almost apologized as he pierced the bamboo pipe with hot iron to make just the right-sized hole in it, taking even greater care that the iron pierced just one side of the pipe and not through and through. He would choose the pipes painstakingly from the bamboo grove he planted himself in his backyard. He made some siphoongs the length of his lower arm, from elbow to wrist. Of course, Ojhai's limbs were short and plump. So these siphoongs were the shortest ones in his collection. And the longest ones he had, ran all the way from his prosperous waist, down to his thick ankle. These he played during Bwisagu, when Birkhang played the kham and Daimalu played the jotha as they teamed up with various dancers and drummers to perform the bagurumba.* And in between these two lengths of siphoong, he made many more with varying lengths and thickness, playing them to suit the varying emotions of his gentle, compassionate and

* Bagurumba is the traditional Bwisagu folksong of the Bodos.

fun-loving heart. Ojhai's sons and daughter-in-law could tell the state of his mind from the siphoong he played by the fire during winter evenings and under the breezy boughs of the flaming gulmohar during the evenings of summer. It was as if he breathed through his siphoong, as if his heart was not within him but in his siphoong. People from villages far and near around Madlagami always thought and spoke of Ojhai and his siphoong as a single entity. They could never imagine Ojhai without his siphoong. Ojhai too could never think of going anywhere without his siphoong tucked into the phali around his waist. Little wonder, then, that children used to call him Abou Siphoong—Grandfather Siphoong!

And Ojhai never sold his siphoongs.

'These are not something you measure with money, Birkhang,' he said. 'These are treasures you give for free to those who play it with all the love in their heart.'

'No barter here?' Birkhang teased.

'Barter, yes. You part with a siphoong and in return you get someone who spreads more flute-notes. Barter, isn't it?'

Birkhang winked. 'Okay, okay, you win. Here's to your siphoong!' And he raised his mug of jou to his lips and took a noisy sip.

Sometimes, when the jou lifted their spirits and loosened their knees, the old men would get up and gently begin swaying to the tunes of the siphoong. Winter's chill and darkness would be falling all around them upon their small Bodo village of Madlagami by the river Jwima. But the cosy, crackling little fire around which Ojhai, Daimalu and Birkhang sat would form a warm halo around the old men, keeping the chill and darkness from reaching them—in body and spirit. 'Feed the fire and it warms your heart in return,' Ojhai would say. During those merry moments, Ojhai would play Bwisagu tunes into his siphoong and Birkhang would no longer be able to control himself. He would take his aronai off his shoulder and, in great zest, tie it around his head before breaking into a joyful bagurumba.

That evening too was one of those spirited times when merry Bwisagu notes from Ojhai's siphoong filled the night air till the edge of Madlagami and beyond the Jwima. Birkhang didn't realize when exactly he unwrapped his green-and-yellow aronai from around his neck and tied it around his head. And suddenly, Bwisagu and a feeling of spring filled Ojhai's yard even in that cold month of January. Soon, Ojhai's siphoong drew others out of their homes to flock around the old men, giving way to an impromptu, boisterous bagurumba around the little fire in the little courtyard. Ojhai paused only for breath in between. During one such break, he said, 'Give the siphoong some wind and it bestows upon you merry company, Birkhang, see?'

'Yes, I see,' Birkhang replied, panting but with no intention to stop dancing yet. And the singing and dancing went on late into the evening.

When the group got tired at last and the night got colder, they stopped to catch their breath. Some came closer to the fire and squatted on the ground. Others said their goodbyes and left.

'Baah! That was one splendid dance I had after ages, Ojhai. It felt so good!' said Daimalu. 'Both my soul and my body are sated!'

'And I, Birkhang, robust, round and ruffian, feel light and lovely as a dove's lone feather swaying gently in the breeze on its way to the ground!' Birkhang said with intense drama, talking of his soaring spirits trying to land back on good earth. The men laughed till tears rolled down their cheeks. Participants kept leaving until only Ojhai, Birkhang and Daimalu were left warming their palms by the fire, which too had ebbed. Ojhai's daughter-in-law brought out three more mugs of jou that evening and lovingly sat a mug beside each old man.

'And this, Ojhai, is one splendid daughter-in-law you have,' said Daimalu, grinning from ear to ear as he picked up the good ale.

Ojhai beamed as he nodded; that beam which came from a gratified heart was further enhanced by the glow of the embers upon his face. The little performance made the blood rush to his cheeks and ears, making them redder. Very soon, when the jou reached his insides, it would redden his small, round nose too. 'Mind, Daimalu,' he said contentedly, 'you only get when you give, depending on what you give and how you give.'

Daimalu nodded. 'Yes, it's all a give and take.'

'Okay, okay, now I know what you'll say next, Ojhai,' Birkhang said with a hearty laugh, slapping his friend on the back.

'Oh yeah? Let's hear it, then, what I'll say in a moment from now, old fortune teller,' Ojhai challenged in jest. 'Go on, predict!'

'Just you watch, Daimalu,' went on Birkhang. 'Our great thinker will now say: "Life is but a barter…"' Birkhang cleared his throat, took another gulp of jou and mimicked Ojhai: 'You give something, you get something in return!'

'Ah ha!' Ojhai smiled. 'And isn't that truly so? You give good, you get good. You give out of love, you get something out of love in return. Money is something, but not everything, you see. In life's many barters, it is your thoughts and deeds that matter. Look for and find precious moments that will warm the nooks of your heart in your old age, like this fire here.'

As the men absorbed what Ojhai said, they suddenly fell pensive and instinctively turned their gaze towards the fire. It indeed warmed the nooks of their hearts. But Daimalu broke the reverie. 'There! There! Talking of barter, have you fellows heard of this age-old fair near Morigaon? The Jonbeel Fair?'*

'What of it?' Ojhai asked, still staring at the embers.

'Trade there is done only through barter, Ojhai. Have you heard about it?'

'Oh! Nwngau! Yes, yes!' Birkhang exclaimed, almost falling off his khamplai—so immense was the force of recollection that hit him at the back of his now-tipsy head, of a story he heard a long time ago. 'Of the Tiwa people, is it, Daimalu? Where the king, the Gobha King, comes down to receive his taxes even now? Nwngau! Nwngau! I've heard of this Jonbeel barter fair, but things seem to have gone somewhat vague. Is the fair still held?' he raised his mug of jou and looked at Daimalu.

'It does,' Daimalu nodded.

Out of sheer excitement, Birkhang exclaimed, 'Come, come then! Let's all three of us visit it once. So which time of the year does this Jonbeel Fair take place? Let's go for the next one, for who knows what happens tomorrow, what give and take of life and death...'

'Sshh! Birkhang, sshh!' Ojhai interrupted. 'I have many more tunes yet to play.'

Meanwhile, Daimalu thought hard, did some mental calculations and replied, 'It takes place ... mm ... well, sometime around the harvest festival in the month of Magh. January.'

'Hey!' Birkhang said excitedly, slapping his thigh. 'But it

---

* *Since over five centuries now, the Jonbeel Fair, organized by the indigenous Tiwa people of Assam, continues to stand out as the only fair where trade is done exclusively on the basis of barter, mainly, though not solely, by tribal people from Assam and Meghalaya.*

is already the month of Magh and the harvest festival isn't too many days from now!'

So, sitting there by the fire on their wooden khamplais, warming their palms and sometimes standing up and turning around to warm their rears, the three old men started making plans to visit the Jonbeel Fair at Doyang Belguri, some distance off the highway in the town of Morigaon.

'But isn't this place very far?' Ojhai wondered aloud.

'It is but not prohibitively so,' Daimalu replied, turning the fish in the embers.

'And what do we expect to find there?' Birkhang asked.

'You're asking, eh? Old man?' Daimalu laughed. 'From dried ginger, fermented fish and roots to heal yellow fever and rejoin broken bones to yam, dried jackfruit seeds and sticky rice, sesame and jaggery. There'll be duck and quail with their eggs. You'll also find our traditional dao, along with every other tool and device our forefathers used, to hunt and cultivate, to weave and build carts and huts. Oh! And straight-out-of-the-loom mekhelas for women, shawls and traditional shirts for men as well. And you know what? There just might be some magic show too. Because, from what I have heard, the ancient land of magic in Assam that goes by the name of Mayong, is not too far from the fair grounds. So, magic practitioners come by to earn a couple of things in kind. Well then, boys, this is all that you may expect to find at the Jonbeel Fair; and some more. All indigenous, all barter.' Daimalu took the mug to his lips once more. This time, he had to tilt it way up, for the divine liquid was almost finishing. Almost. And while he held his upper lip and nose in his mug, making it look like a beak and shaking it so as not to waste even one drop of the divine brew, many oohs and aahs escaped Ojhai and Birkhang as their jaws dropped in awe of the fair.

'Oh, yeah, and you'll find beads and trinkets too,' Daimalu continued after taking the faux beak off his nose. 'Just like the ones our ancestors wore. And all in barter, Ojhai, all in barter!' Daimalu paused, raised his mug and winked. 'And to top it all, there'll be good, home-brewed ale!'

'Let's go then, my friends!' Ojhai announced, raising his siphoong.

'Let's go!' Daimalu raised his mug.

'Let's go!' Birkhang raised an arm and waved his aronai like a victory flag.

And so it was arranged.

Daimalu's son had a friend who hailed from Morigaon. It was from him that Daimalu came to know of the Jonbeel barter fair. It was also through him that Daimalu's son would arrange for the three old men to stay. Ojhai's son volunteered to chaperone the men till Guwahati. He gathered information that, during the days of the fair, buses plied directly from Guwahati to the fair grounds. It was decided that Ojhai's son would seat them in one of those direct buses at Guwahati. At Jonbeel, Daimalu's son's friend would receive them. Almost everything was set. Almost. Only the most important thing remained.

'What shall we barter with?' Ojhai thought aloud. It set the others thinking.

This trip was turning out to be a mega adventure in the lives of the old friends who had never before wished or felt the need to see how the world outside Kokrajhar looked like. And why would they? They found here in their homeland everything that they loved and lived for. Now, however, for this sudden upcoming adventure that jolted them out of their comfort zones and warm khamplais, Ojhai thought long and hard before finally deciding to take a few of his siphoongs to barter with. If someone wished to have a siphoong, he would ask them if they knew how to play it. And even if he really longed for what the other had to barter for a siphoong, he wouldn't, he told himself, strike the deal if the other failed to appreciate the siphoong. Though he believed that there surely would be people out there who would value the worth of a siphoong.

'I shall ask my woman to send some phalis, aronais and dokhonas that she wove herself,' said Birkhang.

And Daimalu was all set to take some sticky rice and a few bamboo hollows stuffed with smoked pork, with the mouth of the bamboo then covered with banana leaves and tied securely with an ultra-thin bamboo split.

By the time the plan fell into place, the mugs had emptied and the men got up to retire for the night. Birkhang and Daimalu each wrapped an arm around the other's shoulder as they walked out of the courtyard into the night, each claiming that the other was tipsy and needed support. Ojhai too got up and walked into the house with a slight falter in his steps, his siphoong on his lips and peace in his heart.

***

So the weekend after Magh Bihu, Ojhai, Birkhang and Daimalu got off the bus at the Jonbeel fair grounds. It was early morning, but the grounds were already starting to fill up. People were pushing bicycles with fat, nylon bags hanging from the handles and fatter sacks saddled on the carrier above the rear wheel. Some pushed in handcarts loaded with jute and wicker baskets, pottery and toys made of clay and wood to barter. Women carried babies tied on their backs with shawls and cattle bells made of copper strung through ropes of grass and reed in their hands. All those footsteps and vehicles raised much dust, but higher than the dust rose the din of voices—of bargaining and vending, of laughter and chatter, people jostling and the tinkling of bicycle bells. There were hollering adults looking for children who had wandered away in the crowd. Birkhang and Daimalu walked through the high, double-way gate into the grounds. Ojhai walked a few paces behind because he was carrying a few of his long siphoongs supported across a shoulder. Several times, when he walked too close, he had jabbed Birkhang on the back with the extending instruments. Nor could he walk beside his friends because on a couple of occasions earlier when he turned to look at the excitement all around him, his long siphoongs had once again swung around and hit Daimalu on the back. During one such swing, the siphoongs had almost hit a young woman's head. Fortunately, she ducked in time. 'Ohoi!' shouted the man accompanying her, 'Mind those sticks!' 'These aren't sticks!' Ojhai retorted, holding back an apology. 'Whatever! Mind them!' the man frowned and walked away. Hence, Ojhai walked a few paces behind, careful not to turn around without looking. So when he approached the gate to the fair grounds, he looked up to read what was written way up on the elaborate awning of the gate, taking extra care to tilt only his head backwards.

'Historic...' Ojhai read the Assamese alphabets slowly but aloud, '...Gobha Dewraja's Jonbeel Mela Gate...' and with each word he pronounced, his back began to tingle with excitement. He was about to witness and be part of one of the most ancient, historic and momentous commercial events ever. It was like a festival. 'Boy!' he said to himself, tightening his grip on his siphoongs and squaring out with pride the shoulders that bore them. His mind wandered towards the hills and forests of these parts of Assam through which the enthralling notes of his siphoongs would soon float. His mind wandered into the villages in those foothills which would hold the siphoongs dear to their hearts. Ah! He felt so ecstatic that his ecstasy drove him to the point of nervousness!

'Ojhai lei! Fwi! Fwi! Come, come!' Daimalu broke his reverie. Birkhang's nostrils meanwhile caught the aroma of crabs being cooked with roselle leaves breezing towards them from somewhere among the handful of foodstalls in the fair. That very instant, Birkhang knew where he would have his midday meal.

Ground space was fast disappearing as people started laying out their wares and putting up their stalls. The three friends positioned themselves next to a garment stall so that they would get some shade from the hanging mekhelas. They spread on the ground the reed mat that Daimalu's son's friend had handed them and sat on it. Looking around, they noticed that agricultural products were displayed by dividing them into equal portions.

'Wouldn't you like to do the same, Daimalu, with your joha and sticky rice?' Birkhang suggested.

Daimalu shook his bald head, 'Nope!'

'Why so?' Birkhang asked.

'It's so,' Daimalu explained with an air of superior intelligence, 'because if I get something of great value to me, then I give more rice; if of less value, I give less rice. It'll be my judgement regarding the amount. No portions. That's all.'

'But how much more or how much less?' Birkhang argued. 'Look! Makes more sense if more is two portions and less is one of such a portion.' Daimalu frowned with mock annoyance as he realized the math and set upon portioning out the rice on the leaf of a banana plant. Birkhang unknotted the corners of the endi shawl in which his wife had wrapped the dokhonas, phalis and aronais, and laid them out neatly on the same shawl upon the ground. Ojhai placed his siphoongs in front of the dokhonas and rice. As the sun rose in the sky, so did the happy commotion and jostle of people at the fair. Just as the three settled down with their wares, a voluptuous lady with a large cloth bag staggered up and plonked herself in front of the dokhonas.

'What, brother, may I offer for one of these?' she asked, placing one hand on the dokhonas and with the other, rummaging through the contents of her bag.

'What do you have to offer?' Birkhang asked.

She took out trinkets of copper, silver and bronze along with strings of brightly coloured beads, strings of rudraksh and tulsi beads, and earrings made from coloured dove feathers.

'Aha! My woman could surely do with one of these,' said Birkhang, taking a pair of silver anklets in his hands.

'Oh! But these should barter for more than a dokhona, brother,' she said. 'How about a phali as well?' After some light-hearted haggling and negotiation, the deal was agreed upon.

'And aren't these siphoongs?' She carefully picked one and turned it around, examining it.

'They are,' Ojhai nodded.

'Wonderful! My aunt's grandson was looking for one. A fine young man that one is. You should hear him whistle into one of these! Sheer magic!'

'Then why don't you take one for him?' Ojhai offered.

'But of course! Why don't I?'

'Take your pick,' Ojhai told her. The woman picked one slightly longer than the shortest one. She then riffled through her wares and, picking up a small but pretty pair of silver earrings, held them out to Ojhai. 'Here, brother, do keep these,' she said. Ojhai gently kept the earrings in his bag for his daughter-in-law.

While the woman was still exchanging with the old friends stories of how Bodo people and villages in the two districts of Morigaon and Kokrajhar were different from each other, an old man walked up to them. He bartered a fishing net for two bamboo hollows of pork and one portion each of joha and sticky rice.

As the morning slipped into noon, the things in the possession of the old friends were fast changing. Two young women came up next, sat in front of them and looked at Ojhai's longest siphoongs—the Bwisagu ones. Ojhai instantly knew how adept one of the women must be at blowing the musical instruments from the way she picked one of the siphoongs and inspected it.

'Go on, blow into it, child. Try it,' he said to the young woman.

'Oh? May I?' she said, pleasantly surprised.

'You may. Go on!' Ojhai smiled.

The woman hesitantly picked the siphoong, very carefully. And when she started playing, it was as if all other din suddenly receded and vanished. Ojhai could now hear only the lilting, dream-like melody that flowed out of his siphoong played by someone other than him. It was a melody that flowed out of passion. Ojhai saw that the woman closed her eyes as she played and was lost in her melody. She was merged with the siphoong.

'Maira!' Her friend nudged her. Maira stopped and opened her eyes. 'Hey, let's go, Maira. Father will be looking for us.' With her soft hands, Maira gently wiped the siphoong where her lips touched it and placed it back on the reed mat.

'Thank you, uncle, it was an honour,' she said, lowering her head towards Ojhai. 'I have always longed for one such, but…'

'But?' Ojhai interrupted. 'What stops you from having this?'

'I have nothing to barter it with,' she said. There was pain in her eyes, the kind that one felt upon separation from a loved one after a very intense but brief moment of togetherness. 'Maira…' Her friend pulled her away.

'Here, Maira!' Ojhai stood up and called after her. He had the siphoong, the one that the young woman longed for, in his hands. 'Take this with you. Now go!'

'But to give in return I have—' Maira stammered.

'Your word,' Ojhai completed for her. 'Promise me that you and the siphoong will together bring joy to others. And if someone with a passion as great as yours wishes to learn the art, you shall impart such learning. Give me your word for this, Maira. You may have the siphoong if you give me your word. And our barter is done.' Saying so, he extended the magic wand to her.

Maira's eyes glistened with tears as she received the siphoong. 'You have my word, uncle!' she choked.

Meanwhile, Ojhai hadn't realized that Birkhang and Daimalu's stuff was all gone, except for a purple phali. Many more people came, inspected the siphoongs, and offered stuff that none of the old men were interested in. So the barters did not fall through. By now, they were starting to get hungry too. Birkhang worried that the crab and roselle curry would get over. Just then another man came and examined the siphoongs. Ojhai in turn gazed at the pea-sized, dark-brown mole sticking on the man's right nostril like a tick sticking to a dog's ear, bloated and succulent from sucking blood.

'So,' he said, 'what shall be the worth of this?' and picked the longest remaining siphoong. 'I have some dolphin-fat oil to massage your aching muscles with, and a measure of star anise. Great spice, that. And yes, a fistful of white cowries too, if fortune telling is in your know-how.'

Ojhai thought for a while and turned to his friends. 'What do you think?' he asked them.

'Guess we could all do with some dolphin-fat massage oil, eh? What say, Birkhang?' Daimalu passed the query on.

'Sure we could, yeah!' Birkhang nodded vigorously.

Ojhai nodded back at his friends and then nodded at the man. How the mole distracted Ojhai each time he looked at him!

'Barter!' the man announced, reaching into his bag and pulling out a two-litre bottle of coke filled with waxy stuff. 'Here's your dolphin,' he said, handing the bottle and taking the siphoong from Ojhai. 'Hah! I mean dolphin-fat oil!' And he guffawed with such great force at his own slip that for a moment Ojhai thought the laughter would shake the mole off his nostril.

'So you play the siphoong?' Ojhai asked.

'So, do I?' he asked back and laughed again.

'Look!' he said, looking Ojhai right in the eyes. 'Does it matter to you? This is a fair and we have all come to exchange our wares. What you do now with the dolphin-fat oil is your business and what I do now with the siphoong is my business. Once the barter is through, my man, isn't it fair that we mind our own wares in our own lives?'

Ojhai was considering handing back the bottle of coke and calling off the barter.

'However,' the man continued, 'this doesn't answer your question. I may know how to play the siphoong; and maybe excellently too.'

Ojhai considered letting the barter take place. But by the time he decided, the man was gone; so was the siphoong.

Ojhai bartered the last siphoong—longer than his forearm but shorter than his longest—for two pairs of ivory bangles for his daughter-in-law. The man who took this last siphoong wore a sleeveless jacket with bright red, black and white horizontal stripes and wooden buttons along the opening in front. His right ear was pierced on top, through which he wore a copper ring.

'So we're done, fellas,' Daimalu stood up. 'Let's pack up and go find some food.'

'Yeah, and then let's take a look around. We haven't yet seen the whole ground,' Birkhang added. 'There's tomorrow too, though. But right now, food! Crab and roselle!' He smacked his lips with such great noise that people around turned to see if some clandestine kissing was afoot. The old men laughed and jostled their way through the milling crowd towards the food stalls. They walked through a crowd of foreigners, some with skin the colour of pale peach and a few as that of ebony. They also passed by journalists who were clicking photos and videos, and taking random sound bytes and interviews. There were a couple of VIPs too, being escorted by uniformed personnel. And there were people, people and more people.

The old men sat for their meal at last, and to Birkhang's utter joy, some crab and roselle curry was still left.

'We accept good money,' said the lady who ran the stall. 'No barter here.'

As the men ate, they heard such enchanting flute notes drifting towards them that Ojhai's hand froze midway between plate and mouth, and his jaw dropped while his ears took in every note. He could make no mistake in recognizing the sound of the siphoongs he made so lovingly. The lady managing the stall approached them to ask if they needed anything. Ojhai looked at her and waved his left hand in the direction where the music was coming from.

'Ah, that!' she smiled indulgently. 'That's my man. He just got himself the kind of siphoong he long wished for and was beside himself with excitement as he came and showed it to me. Yes, that's him. He forgets food and drink when he gets one of them to his lips. He forgets his own self too.' Her words filled Ojhai's heart. It brimmed with a certain joy that he doubted he would find in bartering his siphoongs. He suddenly felt he could eat some more rice! The purpose of his siphoongs had been served.

But which one could it be? Could it be the trinket lady's aunt's grandson? But this was the sound from a long, Bwisagu siphoong. And no, it just couldn't be the mole man. He had shown no passion whatsoever for the siphoong, nor spoken with respect about what he would do with it. Ojhai almost regretted that barter. So, then, could it be the man in the sleeveless jacket and the pierced right ear? Or had Maira gone back on her words and traded the siphoong for something else? Could Maira do that? For a moment, Ojhai's mind lay as confused and crowded as the Jonbeel Fair, trying to figure out the barter of life, the give-and-take that kept life moving. In that instant, he realized, what was indispensable for someone might just be, for another, a medium towards other wants. He wondered, for the first time ever, if he was imposing his passion for the siphoong on anyone and everyone. For, would he ever let the love for copper earrings in a pierced ear be imposed upon himself? He wouldn't.

As the friends came out of the food stall, Daimalu said excitedly, 'I saw him when I went to wash my hands! The lady's husband!' Ojhai stopped in his tracks as Daimalu continued, 'The man with the mole!'

The sun would soon sink into the paddy stumps in the horizon and Daimalu's son's friend would be at the gates of the grounds to take them home. Till then, they decided to walk around and take a look. So, having gone just a few paces, they saw a thin, tall man with his back towards them, haggling over two seeded bananas which he kept referring to as bhimkol. His right hand had some kind of a stick that stuck to his back through the neck of his shirt. And he was scratching his back with it. When he took it out to shoo away the stray dog that walked past, the old men saw that it was a siphoong. Ojhai never made a mistake in recognizing his own. He shivered. Birkhang went up to the man and lightly tapped his shoulder. The man turned and looked up. No, Ojhai had never seen the man earlier; never bartered a siphoong with him.

'So, umm … where did you get this from?' Birkhang asked him, motioning towards the siphoong.

'Does it matter?' he grinned, baring tobacco-stained teeth.

'It does,' Daimalu replied. 'Did you get it from a man in a red, white and black sleeveless cotton jacket? Sporting a copper ring through a pierced ear?'

'Did I?' He looked at the siphoong. 'No, I didn't.'

'Do you know how to play it?' Ojhai asked, slowly sitting beside him.

'Why should I?' he replied, insolence oozing from his words.

'Then why did you barter for it?' Birkhang asked.

'Come on, simple,' he laughed. 'Just so I can barter it away for something else again. It is money in kind.' He again pushed the siphoong through the neck of his shirt to scratch his back.

'But wouldn't you have liked to have a siphoong for the sake of it being a siphoong?' Ojhai asked.

'Look!' he answered. 'Would you like to have money for the sake of it being money?'

Ojhai remained quiet.

The man went on: 'You can't eat money, dear uncle; you can't wear money. You can't create music either with money. You can't love money. And yet, you need money. You know why?'

'Why?' Ojhai asked, looking into his eyes.

'Because it is worth every barter in life. And just so, I don't long for the siphoong for it being a siphoong. I need it only as a medium of barter. That's why!' He took out the siphoong from his back and wiped it on his pants.

Ojhai sighed and took a deep, long breath. Maybe to calm his heart.

'By the way, uncle, do you keep track of where and from whom you receive each currency? Just so with this...' and he shrugged and held up the siphoong.

'Would you barter it with me?' Ojhai asked instinctively.

'For?' he asked.

Ojhai realized he had nothing of value to offer the young man.

'For a purple waist cloth, my man, a phali,' Birkhang chimed in, coming closer to Ojhai and placing a gentle hand on his shoulders. 'That might be of some use to you.'

'Let's see...' The man turned away from the seeded bananas and looked at the purple phali. 'Deal!' he said.

***

Amidst the maddening crowd of the Jonbeel Fair, Ojhai began to feel lost and lonely. He felt a desperate longing to be home in his own little courtyard by the fire, playing his siphoong to himself. Seeing the descending dusk and chill penetrating into Ojhai's heart, Birkhang pulled his aronai off his shoulders and wrapped it around his head. Daimalu picked up the cue and burst into an impromptu bagurumba song, and the two started dancing around Ojhai. In the orange glow of the setting sun, only they noticed the tears that Ojhai was trying to hold back. Birkhang took Ojhai's hand, placed the siphoong in it and raised it to Ojhai's lips.

Later, when Daimalu's son's friend came to pick them, he saw that the fair had winded up for the day and yet, more than half of the people were still there, dancing and singing in the open space in front of the two-way gate. A lazy twirl of smoke rose from the centre of the crowd, and enthralling notes of a siphoong floated out into the dusk from somewhere there. The strains of a bagurumba were making people sway and dance. Daimalu's son's friend shoved his way through the merry group and when he reached the centre, he saw that Birkhang, Daimalu and Ojhai were doing just what they did every winter evening back at home by the fire—recreating the joys of Bwisagu, of spring, even in the cold month of Magh. From the far away hills which were growing dark, notes of another siphoong flowed in and joined Ojhai's notes. Notes of yet another siphoong flowed in from the river down south. Ojhai made no mistake. These were siphoongs he had made. As he closed his eyes and played on, he saw Maira and the mole man playing his siphoongs.

'Life, Birkhang, is still a barter, and a good one!' Ojhai said, smiling.

# Chapter 2

# THE SHAMAN

Ojhai couldn't find his ceremonial siphoongs—three of them.

He remembered very well wrapping them in a soft endi shawl and having left the bundle on a khamplai on the verandah, but he didn't remember at all where he carried it from there. That was a couple of weeks ago. He tried hard to recollect now but just couldn't remember.

'Oi, Ojhai!' Daimalu called from the courtyard. The morning sun had warmed the earth that lay cold and moist from dew the whole of the previous night in the cold month of January. Inside the house, Ojhai pulled out his head from under his bed. He was on his knees and palms, crawling into every cranny he could squeeze himself into, looking for his flutes.

'Ojhai, lei!' Daimalu called out once again. 'Dhanonjoy, Lasit and all are already at work in the fields by the Bathou temple. I saw them on my way here. Hurry! They're waiting for us.'

'Have they planted the Sijou yet?' Ojhai asked. He was still inside the house, but was on his feet now, and lightly clapping his hands to shake off the dust from them.

'They did that some three or four days ago. Oja Bwrai had shown them the exact location to plant it,' Daimalu replied, adjusting the eye holes of the monkey cap on his head. He and the cap had together braved many a winter, clinging on to each other like adolescent lovers.

'And the five-fold bamboo fence around it?' Ojhai asked, emerging from the house.

'That's done too,' Daimalu replied.

'Good!' Ojhai replied. 'I have already spoken with Bibaree,' he said, referring to the shaman. The villagers did not refer to her as a shaman though. They referred to her as the doudini. It was incredible how the quiet and meek, small-statured, almost fragile Bibaree transformed into the confident and incontestable oracle during the kherai rituals. She would start her dance by gently swaying her head, like the raised hood of a cobra, as Oja Bwrai the priest invoked the deity with his chants. As the chanting progressed, the doudini's head would swing faster and faster, making her long, thick hair swish like a hurricane in monsoon. It was incredible too, how within those few hours, that fragile woman acquired the strength to carry the long thungri in one hand and the dhaal in the other. She not just carried them, she swung them around as if they were a dry twig and a paper wheel. Then, when the deity entered the doudini's being, she would speak with the nerve of a lioness with her cubs! And at that moment, she would tell what fortune or misfortune lay ahead for the village and its inhabitants; because it was, in reality, the deity who spoke through her.

'Did you remind Rajesh about the chicken and the pig?' Ojhai asked, slipping his feet into the flip-flops in the verandah.

'Yes, yes, I did,' Daimalu replied, turning towards the gate. 'Let's go now, Ojhai. Birkhang will join us on the way.'

And so Ojhai and Daimalu set out for the fields near the Bathou temple, where young boys of the village were preparing the altar for the year's Kherai Puja, in honour of Bathou. In Madlagami, they observed the Kherai Puja each year on the night of the full moon in the cold month of Magh. The paddy fields were harvested by then; the granaries were full and the villagers were grateful to providence. So they prayed that the gods of abundance and good fortune continued to shower their graces upon Madlagami. On the day of the rituals, Oja Bwrai would hang a piece of new, white cloth woven out of raw, hand-spun yarn upon a tender, green bamboo with leaves to the south of the Sijou plant.

'This,' he would explain subsequently, 'is the obanglaoree. This,' he would narrow down the small slits of his eyes to emphasise his superiority and raising his small round chin with its three black and two white whiskers, say, 'signifies our forefathers, without whom we would not be here where we are; we would not be who we are. And because all our forefathers too have come from the same Creator, that piece of cloth that you see there also flutters to signify the formlessness of the Creator. The cloth will take the form of anything it is wrapped around. Just like Bathou, our Creator, who is in everything in which you look for him, in any form.'

'Then why the Sijou, Abou Oja Bwrai?' a child had once asked.

'Ah, dear little one,' Oja Bwrai had explained, 'it is to give some form to Bathou so that it is easy for little ones like you to close your eyes and have something tangible to think of as Bathou. And that form for us Bodos is a plant, the Sijou plant, which signifies life and growth among our people.' Northward from the Sijou plant, there would be a row of eighteen cord grasses, which Oja Bwrai called the khangkhla plant. Beyond that was the altar of Mainao, the goddess of wealth and abundance.

'Ohoi, there!' Birkhang called. He was approaching from a narrow, side-path through a grove of betel nut palms. The path opened into the fields just next to Ojhai and Daimalu.

'Ha! Slept well and long, eh, old fellow? Look at those puffed-up eyes!' said Daimalu, squinting to look at Birkhang. And the men laughed as their steps fell together towards the Bathou temple.

The winter sun sluggishly pushed its way up through a horizon of fog. As the old men walked through the fields, their bare ankles brushed past the left-over stalks of paddy, still wet from the night's dew on them. A few early cows were chewing on them.

'One thing about this annual Kherai Puja, Daimalu, is that you get to see Bibaree dance in her incarnation as the doudini in such an exhilarating manner … as if she wouldn't get another chance to perform another dance,' Birkhang said. 'I swear by Bathou! She's still amazing! Just like she used to dance the bagurumba when we were all young, remember, Ojhai?'

Ojhai was indeed trying hard to remember but something else—his flutes. If he didn't find them, he would have to play one of his other flutes during the ritual. It saddened him, for never in all these years since he started playing the siphoong during the Kherai Puja did he play any other than one of his three ceremonial flutes. Even as he walked beside Daimalu and Birkhang, his mind searched the corners of his house and his barn. In two more days, the Magh moon would be at its fullest and brightest, and Oja Bwrai would start his chants to invoke the deity into the doudini; into Bibaree. He would require music from the siphoong, kham, jotha and serja to intensify his chants and make the doudini dance. Only then would he be able to entice the deity to descend upon her. Loldong and Birkhang would play the khams that they always did. Daimalu always played the same pair of jotha, the brass cymbals that glistened in the light of the full moon. Every year, on the morning of the Kherai rituals, he polished it with a slice of elephant apple to give it the shine of a mirror. And Koren caressed the strings of the same serja, year after year, so mesmerizingly that he often made the women among the spectators, both old and young, weep and fall in love with him. It didn't matter to those women that he had seen more than five decades of Kherai Puja, and that his hair was turning silver. As for Ojhai, many people from other villages came to the Kherai Puja of Madlagami only to hear him play the siphoong. They wondered whether a second deity descended upon him to create the divine, enchanting melody of his flute. Such was the combined magic of Ojhai and his ceremonial siphoong. But this year, Ojhai didn't know what he would create magic with. All his ceremonial flutes were missing. While his mind raced from place to place in a flashback, trying to recollect and retrace his whereabouts and actions in order to track his flutes, Daimalu continued chatting.

'Remember, Ojhai? How Birkhang once became so enchanted with Bibaree's dance during Bwisagu that he missed the rhythm and forgot to beat his kham?' Saying this, he slapped Birkhang on the back and laughed so hard that drool trailed down the chin of his monkey cap.

'Oh yeah?' Birkhang guffawed. 'And who was so charmed by the dance that he became numb enough for his jotha to fall from his hands?' And the two roared with laughter once again.

Daimalu then sobered down and said, 'And remember? It was the Bwisagu after that when Bibaree suddenly lost her senses while still dancing and fell hard on the ground?'

Receiving no response from Ojhai all this while, Daimalu gave him a nudge with his elbow and repeated, 'Nei, Ojhai, remember that Bwisagu when Bibaree lost consciousness and fell down while dancing?'

'Yeah! Yeah! Nwngou!' Ojhai blurted out, bringing his wandering mind back to the fields. The old men were close to the Bathou temple now, and could hear the young boys talking and singing to energize and warm themselves up. The men could also hear the digging bar go *dhwk dhwk* upon the dry, hard ground as the boys loosened the soil to plant the row of cord grass.

'Oja Bwrai feels that was the exact moment…' Daimalu was saying when Ojhai interrupted him: 'Which moment? When Bibaree lost her senses and fell?'

'Yeah, that,' Daimalu went on. 'That was the exact moment when the deities chose her because during that very moment, the kham, jotha and serja, all were being played to a rising ecstasy just like during the invocation at the Kherai Puja.'

'Yeah, and the siphoong too,' said Ojhai, feeling nostalgic now. 'I was playing it.'

'Hmm, yeah,' Birkhang nodded. 'Her friends had to carry her home.'

Bibaree was in the grip of intermittent fever since that day, till the night of the full moon in the month of the Magh. During the months in between, if she happened to look into someone's eyes while the fever raged, she realized she could read their thoughts, whether from days long past or in the present. And her body would at times go through fits of immense trembling, over which she found that she had no control. Such strange things never occurred earlier, not before that Bwisagu when she lost consciousness while completely losing herself in the bagurumba dance. Gradually, Bibaree began to spend more time praying around the Sijou plant in the northeastern corner of their courtyard. And as she moved around it, she sprinkled water with doubri grass from a small earthen pot. Also, whenever she heard the siphoong, kham, jotha and serja all playing at once, even without her realizing it, her body would begin to sway to their rhythm till she eventually broke into a dance. It was a couple of years later that Oja Bwrai realized that Bibaree had become a doudini—shaman.

'She looked fetching in her youth,' Daimalu continued talking, 'didn't she?' Birkhang nodded but Ojhai failed to respond once more.

'And remember? So many asked for her hand!' Birkhang recollected.

'I do. Eh, one came from the town of Kokrajhar too,' Daimalu chimed in. 'Gosh! He arrived astride a motorcycle, remember? Bah! Wealthy fellow he was.' A moment of silence followed.

'She never got married,' Ojhai spoke after a while.

The three friends had reached the temple. From the adjacent mist-filmed pond, a cackle of whistling teals took flight, raising a happy cacophony as they soared into the pale blue, cloudless winter sky. Their cackle made Ojhai look up. The sky above was slowly turning brighter and warmer. As Ojhai continued gazing at the birds, the sound of their wings beating against their soft, feathered bodies reminded him of the sound of the thick, starched dokhona beating against the ankles of the wearer. Maybe Bibaree's ankles, decades ago.

'Fwi, Abou, fwi! Come, grandfather! We're almost done!' one of the young boys called out. They were working with great zeal, preparing for the annual event. Everything had to be meticulously done, otherwise the deity might take offence. And if that happened, Madlagami would be doomed. During the ritual, the young boys would dance with the doudini. Even after the ritual got over, they would continue to sing, dance and make merry till late into the full moon night. Of course, for energy, they would all have sips of the sweet, intoxicating joubidei.

'Good job, boys!' Daimalu lauded their efforts.

'The thungri and the dhaal are at Oja Bwrai's,' Birkhang said. 'He will bring them on the day of the ritual.'

'How fat is the sacrificial pig, Abou?' one of the boys asked with glee, smacking his lips in anticipation.

'Eh, greedy pig, you!' Another lightly kicked him in the butt and he feigned toppling to the ground, laughing. Everyone laughed; all were in great spirits.

Ojhai laughed too. But deep within, his conscience felt heavy. Everything and everyone was ready for the Kherai Puja, except him. Without his ceremonial siphoong, he would not be able to play with all his heart and soul. He would not be able to immerse himself completely in his musical offering to Bathou. The greater fear that engulfed him was that if his devotion and offering weren't whole, the deity might not enter the doudini. Then the whole Kherai Puja and everyone's enthusiasm would go to waste. And he alone would be to blame for it. The village may even be deprived of its blessings, thanks to an unappeased Bathou. Worse still, the village folks might incur Bathou's wrath. Then too, he alone would be responsible for everything. While in person Ojhai remained in the temple yard with his friends and the other village elders to oversee the preparations, in his mind, he was racing to every nook, bag and trunk at home, rummaging through them, wondering where the ceremonial flutes might be.

Ojhai couldn't sleep the night before the full moon and the Kherai Puja. He tossed about in bed. Before the inside of thc thin quilt of simul cotton grew warm against his body, he would roll over to the other side, making it cold all over again. This made sleep elude him all the more. And wakefulness kept heaping guilt onto his conscience. How could he be so careless, he wondered, exasperated by himself. He was letting down his village folks; he was letting down the doudini and Bathou. He kept wondering where the siphoongs might be. They could not be stolen because everyone in Madlagami considered them sacred. In his mind, he vividly saw the endi shawl bundled with the siphoongs lying on the khamplai in the verandah. And yet, in his part-wakefulness and part-anxiety, he didn't see the verandah as vividly. Slowly, somewhere in that in-between state, sleep eventually claimed him. In his dream, the doudini appeared to him and was telling him something, though he couldn't understand what. He knew the figure in his dream to be the doudini, but he saw her as Bibaree of the olden days dancing the bagurumba. Then he saw her losing consciousness and falling hard on the ground. It startled him even then, in his sleep, as it did all those years ago. He woke up with a start. It was still dark outside. The white-throated night jar was croaking out its long but punctuated song from the jackfruit tree outside his window, as it always did. How it tore through the chilly night! It took some time for Ojhai's senses to bring himself out of the bagurumba and remember that it was the day of the Kherai Puja. He sat up in bed. Oja

Bwrai had wanted all of them to gather by afternoon at the altar near the Bathou temple to start the preparations. The main rituals, however, would begin only by nightfall, when the full moon of Magh rose in the night sky. Ojhai flipped the quilt aside, lifted the edge of the mosquito net that hung over his bed and stepped out.

His ceremonial siphoongs were still missing. He would have to play a different one that night.

Towards dusk, a beautiful, round Magh moon began getting brighter against the deep, dark blue of the Madlagami sky. Below it, a few kerosene lanterns and earthen lamps around the Sijou plant washed the puja ground with a mellow light, bright enough for the rituals to begin yet not so much as to take away their mystique. Villagers were already flocking around the Sijou, wrapped in shawls of endi, wool and even cotton. Some had tied little children to their backs using the shawls. Bibaree was sitting calmly near the Sijou. She would not remain calm for long. The elderly and the wise men of the village, the medicine-man and the priests were all present, for each of them had a role to play in transporting the doudini into a trance. They would all assist Oja Bwrai. At a distance, the sacrificial pig was tied using a grass rope around its large, hanging belly to the thin, straight trunk of a betel nut palm. To another palm close to it was tied a healthy rooster by its leg. A few children covered their mouths with their hands and laughed into it, tickled by the idea of the thin trunk keeping such a fat pig from running away. The pig snorted back, much to the merriment of the children.

Oja Bwrai knelt in front of the Sijou and let his head touch the ground. Today, he had a green aronai neatly wrapped around his head like a headgear. Despite the cold, he had on him only a vest. Its sleeves came almost to his elbows and that was all. Even in that old age, he didn't seem to mind the cold at all. Old Rongjalee lit the earthen lamps and Oja Bwrai picked one with reverence and placed it on a small piece of banana leaf inside the low bamboo fencing, at the foot of the Sijou. That very instant, Birkhang and Loldong together started beating their long drums as they called out loudly: 'Jai Bathou Bwrai!'

'Jai!' shouted the villagers in response.

'Jai Bathou Bwrai!' cried Koren as he began picking at the strings of his serja.

'Jai!' the villagers shouted.

'Jai Bathou Bwrai!' called out Holiram as he and Daimalu brought their gleaming pairs of jotha together, clapping them in rhythm with the serja and the drums.

'Jai!' shouted the villagers once again. As the hails rose into the nocturnal air, an uncanny aura of fear and reverence fell around the Bathou temple and the yard of the Kherai Puja. The shouting and hails also aroused in them enough courage to withstand the chill under the open night sky of January.

'Jai!' they all shouted in unison once more. 'Jai! Bathou Bwrai, Jai!'

Only then did Ojhai bring his siphoong to his lips. His heart ached and his mind was restless. But then he remembered what his daughter-in-law had said earlier in the day. 'Why, Apha,' she had said, 'if you play with devotion, any siphoong that you play will become a ceremonial siphoong. And devotion, Apha, lies in your heart. Not in your siphoong.'

Ojhai closed his eyes and, in his mind, he told Bathou: 'If my devotion is true, Bathou Bwrai, I will still get to play one of my ceremonial siphoongs for you tonight.' Yet, the thought made him weep inside, for that was now no more possible. The rituals had begun and there was still no inkling of the whereabouts of his most prized siphoongs. As Ojhai whistled into the flute, a drop of tear rose from his heart to reach his eye and trickled down to land on the flute. And music rose.

'He, whom we call Bathou,' Oja Bwrai began his sermon to a perfectly quiet, motley group of villagers. 'His name stands for the five most profound elements of Creation. Ba, meaning five and gathou, meaning profound. And these five elements, which govern the followers of the Bathou faith, are the sky, fire, air, water and earth. It is, my good folks, these five elements that make up the mortal bodies of flesh and blood that house our souls. And when the soul leaves its house, it is to these same elements that the soul goes back to. The soul itself is air, which is again just one of those elements.' Oja Bwrai had a captivating way of narrating the philosophies of life. He made it sound like a fairy tale, full of intrigue and yet something that the simple villagers were part of. They sat listening in complete awe as Oja Bwrai went on. 'Even the principles that our lives are ruled by are five. They begin with birth. That is the first principle. Then you go through marriage, the enjoyment of family life, then prayer and solidarity for the sick and needy. And finally, it all leads to the ultimate truth of life—death.' He paused, looked around and asked, 'Now let me make it simpler. These five principles are birth, marriage, family life, prayer and solidarity, and finally, death.' And then he sang a beautiful hymn, explaining the significance the Bodos attached to the number five.

Thaigir ni bikhonga khong ba
Sijou ni siria siri ba
Siphoong ni gudunga gudung ba
Bodoni asara asar ba
Bodo Bwraini raoabw phong ba

*The elephant apple has five rinds,*
*The Sijou plant has five rinds,*
*The siphoong has holes five,*
*So do Bodos have principles five.*
*The Bodo priest's preachings too are essentialy five.*

'And to that very Bathou of such limitless kindness, my dear folks, we bow!' Ojhai let the strains of his siphoong rise and fall in lucid waves, allowing the perfect, captivating rise to fill the pauses during the priest's sermons and making his flute let out a low, soothing croon in the background when the priest was talking. Oja Bwrai would talk, ask and seek on behalf of the villagers. The people would speak through him. And the deity would speak through the doudini.

Having thus set the mood, Oja Bwrai began his invocation to the music from the siphoong, khams, jotha and the serja.

Oi Pipha guru
Anan gosai binan gosai nwng!

Bibaree had by now got up and begun to move her head to the pulsating rhythm of the khams. She would soon begin to dance the kherai, which would include eighteen different dance forms. And all of those dance forms came naturally to her. That evening, she wore a blood-red dokhona. Her long hair fell loose upto her thighs and she gently swayed the thungri and the dhaal as she began dancing around the Sijou and the row of khangkhla.

Oja Bwrai continued to charm the doudini into a trance and to invoke the deity.

*O God, our Father!*
*Protect your ignorant children!*

*You are the creator, preserver and destroyer,*
*All in one.*
*Have mercy on your children,*
*Steeped in the darkness of ignorance.*
*Bring us to light, Father,*
*Shower on us your love,*
*O God, be merciful!*

When he had almost finished the first part of his invocation, Bibaree came very close to Ojhai, stared at him and his siphoong, and danced her way back to Oja Bwrai. And gesturing at Dhanonjoy, she called out, 'Nei, Sengra!' Her voice was no longer the soft, gentle, submissive one belonging to Bibaree. It was changing as the transition was taking place. It was different now: crisp and authoritative. Sometimes it was hoarse, sometimes it was high-pitched, but always loud and clear, almost masculine, even though the doudini's transition into the goddess was yet only partial. Dhanonjoy quickly fell to his knees and bowed his head.

'Yes, Mother!' he replied, gripped with the sudden fear that he might have unknowingly offended the doudini.

'Get up, young man,' the doudini spoke, 'and run along right away to Oja Bwrai's chicken coop at the back of his kitchen. One of Ojhai's ceremonial siphoongs lies along its edges, covered under a film of rice husk and chicken droppings. Hurry, lad, hurry! Go fetch it!' Then, without looking at anyone else, she danced her way back to the row of khangkhla plants.

Dhanonjoy sprinted towards the priest's house without a moment's delay. The house was right next to the Bathou temple, but the path lay around the pond. Ojhai's jaw dropped and the siphoong came off his lips. *But how did the bundle reach Oja Bwrai's house?* Ojhai wondered. And as if she read his thoughts, the doudini turned around and, pointing at Ojhai with her thungri, spoke aloud: 'The siphoong player over there! Bundled in an endi shawl, he left three of his siphoongs...' she paused, shook her head as if to bring up the details that had sunk to the bottom of her head, and resumed, 'in Oja Bwrai's verandah, on his way back home from playing them at Bathou's shrine.'

An 'Oh!' escaped Ojhai's lips. Now he realized why the verandah he saw in his dreams wasn't as vivid as the endi bundle; wasn't as familiar as his own verandah. He also recalled how he walked the priest home from the temple with the bundle under his arm. And when Oja Bwrai's daughter-in-law had served tea and rice cakes, he had placed the bundle on the khamplai to go and wash by the well before eating the snacks. While returning, he had forgotten them there and walked back home alone.

Meanwhile, Dhanonjoy felt his way in the dark like a thief towards the chicken coop. How he wished he brought a lantern! The thick foliage of the large mango tree in Oja Bwrai's backyard didn't let any of the light from the full moon reach Dhanonjoy. The repugnant stink of chicken droppings made him feel nauseated. A few chickens crooned low and long, sensing an unexpected human in the vicinity. When he reached the coop, he dropped to his knees and felt the ground around the coop with his bare palms. Dry granules of droppings flattened at his touch. He winced. But he felt on. He kept wondering: *How on earth did Abou Siphoong's flute get here?*

Back in the ritual grounds, as if in response to Dhanonjoy's thoughts, Bibaree smiled tenderly at a little boy dozing in his mother's lap in the crowd. 'Oja Bwrai's little grandson picked the bundle of siphoongs from the khamplai and unwrapped it,' she began to tell the puja attendees, 'and was looking at them with great curiosity when chickens pecking at insects in the courtyard came near him, eyeing his bowl of puffed rice.' People listened to her in awe and she went on: 'So the child picked up a siphoong and, raising it like a stick, shooed the chickens with it and chased them back towards the coop. When the chickens fled beyond the coop and the purpose of the siphoong was over for the child, he dropped it there and returned to his bowl of puffed rice. Over the next few days, rice husk feed and chicken droppings covered it from sight.'

Ojhai's head reeled from disbelief. He dropped it onto his palms and sat down on the cold earth.

Meanwhile, a buzz began in the outer circle of the villagers around the Sijou. It soon grew louder and rolled inwards, towards Ojhai. People turned around to look and, as they parted to make way, Dhanonjoy emerged, sweating through his pullover. In his hand was one of Ojhai's long ceremonial siphoongs!

'Bring it here, lad,' the doudini said, without turning to look at Dhanonjoy. When he took it to her, she sprinkled some water with basil leaves from the little pot at the altar, on the siphoong. She then called Ojhai. 'Hoi, old man! Come take this and play one of your kherai tunes for me!'

As he took the siphoong from her, Ojhai remembered what he had said to Bathou just a few moments ago: 'If my devotion is true, Bathou Bwrai, I will still play one of my ceremonial siphoongs.' Ojhai kept his head bent and his eyes lowered until the doudini said, 'Look into my eyes, Ojhai, look at me!'

Ojhai looked up. Suddenly, he didn't see the woman in front of him as the doudini. He saw her as Bibaree. Of earlier times. She smiled at him. 'You pined for her, didn't you?' She asked him. Ojhai froze. 'Go play your tune now!' she commanded. And suddenly, he once more saw her as the doudini before him.

As the night grew and the moon rose higher into the sky, notes from Ojhai's ceremonial siphoong, the jotha, khams and the serja filled every inch of earth and every speck of sky in Madlagami. The doudini's dance was getting more feverish. Her head moved like it was possessed and she flung her hair around as if she were beating the devil away with it. By now, Oja Bwrai had sacrificed the rooster at Bathou's altar and placed its head along with an earthen bowl full of its blood under the Sijou inside the small bamboo fence. The youngest children at the ceremony began to cry. So the mothers carried them back home and sang lullabies and suckled them to sleep.

The doudini was in a complete trance, her transition from human to goddess complete.

'Hoi, Sengra!' she called out to no one in particular. A young boy came running and knelt in front of her.

'Run to the haystack next to Oja Bwrai's barn. On its eastern wall leans an old bicycle tyre. Facing that tyre, stuck into the haystack, is another of Ojhai's siphoongs.'

This time, Ojhai did not stop playing. He and the rest of the musicians carried on. 'Oja Bwrai's grandson wheeled the bicycle tyre with the siphoong across the courtyard, towards the haystack. And when he got tired playing by himself, he left the tyre there and stuck the siphoong into the haystack.'

Dhanonjoy accompanied the young boy in his quest for the siphoong. This time, they remembered to carry a lantern as they walked through the fog and the dark. The little insects trying to fly across the pond towards the light of the ritual grounds got confused seeing the light of Dhanonjoy's lantern reflecting in the waters of the pond. Getting drawn to it, they dropped into the water, creating tiny concentric circles. In the stillness of the night under the full moon, they made the water seem possessed. Scared, the young boy came closer to Dhanonjoy to walk behind him.

The doudini had by now finished the ranphagli kherai dance, which she did in honour of the goddess of war. She put down the thungri and the dhaal, and Oja Bwrai placed the pot of water from the altar into her hands once again. She now began sprinkling the tulsi-leaves-infused water from the pot and danced around the khangkhla plants, while Oja Bwrai continued with his chants, this time invoking Mainao, the goddess of crops and wealth.

Nwng fwi nangwn, Mainao Ai
Nwng nwnga bla
Jwng bwrei thang nanei thanw
Nwng phwithar nanggwn, Ai
Jwngni phwthar arw bakriao tha fwi Ai

*You must come, Mother Mainao.*
*Without you, how are we to survive?*
*Our very existence rests upon you, Mother Mainao,*
*We beg you, please come!*
*And dwell upon our fields and granaries.*

Meanwhile, the pig too was sacrificed. A pot of its blood and its head were placed at the altar of Mainao. The sensuous fragrance of burning incense, flowers, and the intoxicating aroma of joubidei lifted the senses to a spiritually euphoric sphere. When even mere mortals were induced into such a state of ecstasy, heightened by the gradually rising pace of the music, no wonder the doudini was no more herself. Mainao had descended upon her. She seemed to be pleased with the prayers and sacrifice offered to her.

'Hoi, phisaphwr! Nwngswr angkho mabeao langnw?' she asked, going around the khangkhla plants. Her voice cracked every now and then. 'Hoi, children! Where do you wish to take me? But if you ill-treat me, I shall return the very way that I came.'

Through his chants, Oja Bwrai cajoled and beseeched with the deity in the doudini and at last, the deity agreed to stay in Madlagami's granaries and fields. Oja Bwrai took the pot from her hands and motioned the others to come and stand very close to her, behind her. The music was reaching a crescendo. She suddenly turned around, looked at Oja Bwrai and said, 'Follow your mongrel after sunrise tomorrow. He will lead you to where he had buried a piece of bone from a goat.' The doudini spoke with great rapidity, unlike the unhurried, mild pace that belonged to Bibaree. 'To its left, not too deep into the soil, your grandson has buried the last of Ojhai's missing siphoongs, having learnt to do so from the pet mongrel. He hoped to dig it out later. But tender of age that he is, he has forgotten about it.' She paused and let out a tremendous heave of a breath and said, 'The child's mother has neatly folded old Ojhai's endi shawl and hung it upon her father-in-law's cloth horse, thinking the shawl to be his.'

Then, abruptly, the doudini jerked and turned her head towards the Sijou, swinging her hair all over her face. She then stretched her arms towards the two tender bamboos stuck on the ground on either side of the small fence around the plant and gripped one with each hand for support, still standing and trembling. But the moment she clasped the poles, her head suddenly dropped back and consciousness momentarily left her.

With that, the deity too left the doudini. As the trance lifted, so did the memory of all that she foretold and preached. She would not recall any of it later.

'Hold! Hold!' Oja Bwrai whispered to the people who were standing behind the doudini. They were ready for her transition back into Bibaree and held her as she dropped down.

Loldong and Birkhang struck their khams for one last time for the night. And what a thunderous strike that was! It seemed to have burst open the night to let the deity soar back to her abode in the heavens. Koren too slowly lowered his serja and brought it to rest. Gently, Oja Bwrai sprinkled some water on the doudini's head to bring her back to her human, mortal senses. The heady kherai dance and the Kherai Puja were over. Loldong, Birkhang, Daimalu and Koren were putting the drums, cymbals and serja away.

But Ojhai remained oblivious to it all. With his eyes closed, he continued to remain immersed in playing his ceremonial siphoong with its five holes—the bagathou of his very existence. And inside his closed eyes, he saw a similar heady dance of long ago, a similar euphoric music rising to a crescendo and then all of a sudden, the dancer losing consciousness and dropping to the ground. Bibaree.

When Ojhai's eyes opened, he instead saw the doudini, coming round to her senses. He brought the siphoong away from his lips and looked down at it.

The doudini had returned his lost love.

# Chapter 3

# ORBS OF FIRE

Ojhai liberated a resounding, rolling belch into the night air, sending Birkhang into fits of chuckles. 'Eh, Ojhai! That smelt of the pork and bamboo shoot curry,' he said.

As laughter shook Ojhai's insides, another bellyful of air spiralled up through his guts and with great glee exhaled itself out through the mouth, this time bringing up the aroma of home-bred chicken cooked in a gravy of riceflour and flavoured with kharei. 'Habab! Now that's ondla ingkhri!' Birkhang said, slapping Ojhai on the back as he chuckled once more. 'But I tell you, Ojhai, this was one of the finest wedding feasts we've had in recent times, wasn't it?'

'It sure was, yeah! It was!' Ojhai nodded. 'And the jou! Ah, such sweetness!' Ojhai smacked his lips at the very thought of the rice beer having caressed his mouth.

A sparkle of fireflies moved along with them, above their heads, as if showing the way to the old men in their walk back home across the fallow field. Stars twinkled in the autumn sky, looking like fireflies in heaven, playing hide and seek among tufts of clouds that hung like giant popcorn. Every now and then, a cool, mild breeze tickled the skin to erupt into goose bumps. Both Ojhai and Birkhang were in their best dhotis that day. Ojhai wore a soft blue, full-sleeved kurta over the dhoti. Earlier in the afternoon, when they set out for the wedding in the village of Serfanguri, he had around his neck a red aronai with a pattern of bright yellow flowers woven into it. This was a very special aronai for Ojhai, for he had received it at a Bwisagu celebration many years ago, when he was felicitated for playing the siphoong like no one else in all the villages that side of the river Jwima. No wonder, hence, that he wore this special aronai only during special occasions. And that day's occasion was indeed special to him and to Birkhang as well. For it was the wedding of the youngest daughter of their school mate, Kulin. But now, as they walked across the field, he unwrapped the aronai from his neck and tied it around his waist and tucked his siphoong into it.

As the old men were returning from the wedding feast, there was no one else either within sight or within hearing till far, far away. Silhouettes of aged, grandfather trees stuck out their heads into the dark sky while their branches reached out for the popcorn clouds. Whenever Ojhai, Birkhang and Daimalu had to go anywhere outside their village of Madlagami, they had to walk past this field. That day, though, Daimalu was home nursing a sprained ankle. They knew these fields like the back of their hands. They could close their eyes and tell how many steps ahead the next tree was, which shrubs were on the left and whose paddy fields rolled out on the right. In this stretch of the field, the trees were few and far between. Sometimes in the afternoons, young boys from

Madlagami and a couple of adjoining villages gathered there to play football. At times, they played cricket too. But now as Ojhai and Birkhang passed through it, there was no one except the fireflies leading them. The two old men walked on quietly because their stomachs felt too heavy from the wedding feast for casual talk. Besides the occasional shrill cry of the cicada tearing through the darkness, the night was as still and stealthy as a hidden leopard in the moments before it pounced on its prey.

Suddenly, an owl hooted.

'AAYEII!' Birkhang screamed instantly, jumping up with a start and almost falling over Ojhai.

'Oh? So you're frightened, eh, Birkhang?' Ojhai asked, his hand instinctively reaching for the siphoong at his waist, lest Birkhang broke it. Birkhang hurriedly steadied himself and grinned sheepishly. 'Frightened? Who, me? Bah! I give two hoots to that hoot, Ojhai!'

'Is that so? I can see that!' Ojhai teased.

Birkhang shook his head furiously. 'Frightened, my foot! I was only coming close to hold you, thinking your knees might give way out of fright.' Saying this, he picked up the hem of his kurta, took it to his forehead and wiped it, though it was neither the season nor the hour for droplets of sweat to ooze. And he started a conversation to tide over the stillness of the night.

'So, er, Ojhai, that talkative old man sitting next to you, the one who had this big, black mole with a single white hair bursting out of it; I don't seem to remember seeing him around here before,' Birkhang stated, as fear raced up and down his spine and round and round his intestines. He nervously hoped Ojhai would pick up the conversation and go on talking to fill the silence, just so another sudden noise in the dark would not startle him to embarrassment once more. He would not, he thought, be able to cook up another excuse for more such petrified reactions. Sometimes a dry, fallen stalk of some bush crackled under their sandals but with that he was alright. They were now walking past Braujen's fields.

'Ah, him,' Ojhai replied. 'That was Madhav, the groom's mother's uncle. He doesn't stay around here. His village is somewhere on the south bank of the river Brahmaputra.'

'O ho ho, yes, yes, now it comes to my silly mind. Moirabari or some name like that, eh?' Birkhang asked, turning towards Ojhai, hoping he would speak, rather than making do with a mere nod.

'Yes,' Ojhai replied, 'Moirabari. Far, very far from here.'

'Good that it's far, very far from here,' sighed Birkhang, his heart a wee bit calmed.

'But why?' Ojhai asked, turning towards him.

'Well,' Birkhang hesitated, 'because I don't want the mysterious ghost fireballs hopping from tree to tree around *here* the way they do in his village.'

'Oh! The owrthopla?' Ojhai asked, lightly blowing away a firefly that landed on Birkhang's shoulder. 'The bundle of fire?'

'Yeah, yeah, that. Whatever was Madhav saying about that thing?'

Balls of fire. Live fire—that was what Madhav was talking about during the feast at the wedding. They suddenly appeared on a tree and then leapt away from it to another tree, sometimes several metres away. Then they disappeared once more, only to show up on some different, unsuspecting tree. That was what Madhav was regaling people with. Giddiness from the heady, intoxicating jou was making him fly as loftily as the balls of fire he was describing. The exuberance with which he ate, drank and spoke betrayed his advancing age. And just like his balls of fire, bits of food flew out of his mouth and disappeared as he spoke and chewed simultaneously and voraciously, only to land, a moment later, on the plates and faces of those sitting around him. Ojhai too had been the beneficiary of quite a few such bits of food.

Daylight and the merry wedding crowd, the drums, trumpets and flutes and, most of all, an obscenely scrumptious feast had kept the chill of fright from crawling up Birkhang's limbs and spine when Madhav was speaking about the owrthopla earlier in the day. But now, with darkness all around him and only the quiet Ojhai in place of the merry, boisterous wedding crowd, with croaking bush crickets, cicadas and hooting owls in place of trumpets and drums, a sense of eeriness at the thought of the fireballs suddenly grew and grew till it grew larger than Birkhang's mortified heart and loomed above him. His eyes travelled to the lone siphoong at Ojhai's waist, and he desperately hoped that it would remain unplayed.

'Heck!' he whispered, spitting on the ground. 'They follow people? These fireballs?'

'Madhav didn't say anything about that,' Ojhai replied calmly.

The men walked on in silence for a while. Birkhang looked up and was grateful for the fireflies still hovering above and following them. As the night advanced, the air grew stiller, and the chirp of crickets and cicadas grew louder, firing the imagination to carve weird unicorns and dragons out of the shapes and shadows of the night.

'But Birkhang,' Ojhai broke the silence. 'I just realized, the owrthopla is the same as our Haraibankha.'

'Sshh! Ojhai,' Birkhang brought his mouth very close to Ojhai's ear and whispered into it. 'Sshh! These fields, you know, might have them floating around.'

'Them?' Ojhai wondered aloud, moving his head only slightly away from Birkhang's mouth.

'Them, yeah!' Birkhang almost fell on Ojhai's shoulder to once more bring his mouth close to his ear. 'Them. Spirits!' Having said the word, he moved his mouth away but continued in hushed tones: 'If they hear their name being called, Ojhai, they'll respond and come to follow you home.'

'But the Haraibankha harms no one, Birkhang, and don't you remember ... that instance when Rajen saw them? It was towards dawn and there was enough light to see till far. Rajen saw them from the window of his kitchen.' Ojhai could hear Birkhang gulp. 'And there was more than one, Rajen had said. They appeared atop different trees, flew out to other trees and disappeared, only to reappear elsewhere.'

Birkhang turned around to peer through the darkness. He didn't raise his head but moved only his eyeballs to search the tops and branches of the trees nearest to them.

'Let's walk faster, Ojhai!' he said, panicking.

Ojhai drew out the flute from the aronai round his waist and said, 'Why, Birkhang, let me take your mind off the Haraibankha.' As he closed his eyes and took the siphoong to his lips, Birkhang almost jumped out of his sandals and his hands sprang to reach Ojhai's arms and bring them down, along with the siphoong.

With his voice lowered to as hushed as one can bring a scream to, he blurted, 'Ojhai! No, don't! Are you insane or what? Gone crazy? Don't you know that lilting flute notes in the still of the night catch their attention? For the sake of Bathou Bwrai, have mercy on me, Ojhai. For once, please put the siphoong away. Please do!'

'Hey, hold on! Hold on!' Ojhai said, raising his arms to save his siphoong. 'But what if I play a merry note? Look,

Birkhang, it'll cheer you up and also cheer up the darkness or whatever lurks therein.'

But Birkhang was not to be calmed. 'Ojhai, please. If you truly are my friend and if you truly wish to bring me joy, do just quicken your pace homewards. I'm already sweating and freezing in my dhoti. You don't want me to wet it too, do you?' He wasn't joking. Ojhai sensed this and felt sorry for his friend. He placed the siphoong back into the tuck of the aronai and put his arm round Birkhang's shoulders. And thus they walked on quietly across the field.

As the old men trod through the night, the narrow foot track gradually inched in towards the tall trees. The soft whistling of the breeze through them sounded as if they were escaping from a hundred siphoongs. Ojhai and Birkhang's feet searched out the track and their steps fell on their own along it—more out of familiarity than from actually seeing the path. As they drew closer to the trees, the fireflies still flew with them but decided to do so along the clearing. So instead of flying above their heads, they were now moving alongside. However, a few of them did close in around their ears and hair every now and then. One particular firefly threw such an exceptional glow on Ojhai's face that it made Birkhang turn to look first at Ojhai's cheek, which had suddenly lit up, and then at the source of the light.

'Habab!' Birkhang exclaimed, looking up. 'Now that's a giant of a firefly. Ojhai, look! Look!'

Ojhai looked up. Both the men remained staring at the giant firefly for a moment when realization suddenly dawned on them and their gaze dropped down to each other's eyes at the same instant, and both gasped together, 'HARAIBANKHA!'

Birkhang froze. His jaw dropped and his mouth opened to the widest it could stretch. He thought he let out a terrible scream, but in reality, it got stuck in his throat. Ojhai quickly put his hand on Birkhang's mouth to close it, and looking straight into his eyes, shook his head, gesturing not to make any noise. Birkhang understood and nodded, though his mouth remained agape. He rolled his eyeballs once more to look up without moving his head. The haraibankha had vanished. Just as a sigh of relief was halfway out of his still open mouth, and just as he took off his aronai from his shoulders to wipe the beads of sweat upon his reddened nose, he saw Ojhai's face glowing up again. This time he knew better than to emit a muted scream and choke himself. Instead, he caught hold of one end of the aronai and without looking up, swirled the other end, converting all his fright into muscle power to hit the haraibankha like he would dowse a fire with a jute sack soaked in water. As the aronai slapped the fireball, tiny sparks flew out from it into the darkness, but no change came over it. It was far from dying out. Birkhang continued to lift his aronai again and again and beat the big, hopping ball of fire repeatedly. Each time he did so, more sparks flew out of it, but the haraibankha never lost an iota of its flame. Rather, it danced and bounced with renewed vigour with each swat of the aronai.

It was now Ojhai's turn to find his mouth opening wide out of shock as he watched this bizarre show against the dark sky. He didn't know whether it was divine, satanic or plain sorcery. Instinctively, one of his hands reached down to his siphoong and the other covered his mouth. He looked at Birkhang, shook his head and formed a 'no' with his lips, forgetting that he had his hand over those lips, covering them. Birkhang anyway wasn't throwing even a single glance at him, so frantically was he beating up the haraibankha. His was the kind of energy that could be instigated and aroused only under fright about being taken captive by those from a paranormal dimension. And to Ojhai's horror, the tiny sparks got together to form more haraibankhas—smaller ones. Then a few of the smaller haraibankhas got together and formed bigger ones. Ojhai looked on, stupefied. A few of the fireballs hopped off towards the treetops and vanished, only to reappear close by. These too were now becoming more restless and moved with jerks of greater intensity. Ojhai had to stop Birkhang from swatting the fireballs. So he lunged up and caught hold of the free end of Birkhang's aronai and pulled it down. He then tried to snatch it from him, but Birkhang wouldn't let go.

'Leave, Birkhang. Leave the aronai! Don't be a fool!' he said in a low voice.

But Birkhang was indignant and tugged harder at the aronai.

'I can't, Ojhai!' he said, his eyes red with terror and his lips quivering. 'If I stop now, they'll be all over me! They'll singe me!' His voice grew louder and louder, breaking up in between, till he almost started crying. 'The haraibankhas will burn me, Ojhai, they'll burn both of us! They'll swallow us alive!'

'Sshh! Sshh!' Ojhai tried to pacify him. 'Calm down, my friend, calm down!'

But by this time even Ojhai's heart was no longer calm. He could hear it thudding loudly inside his kurta. The tug of war with the aronai went on and, in the melee, the old men's feet lost track of which way they were going. While their eyes were trying to focus on the many haraibankhas and their hands were trying to focus on the aronai, their feet were hopelessly trying to stay on the right track homeward. In the process, none of their senses worked in tandem with the other and so they soon started going in circles and zigzags. But never homewards—no more. Ojhai realized this only when his gaze suddenly fell on a bush by the wayside, past which they had walked a while ago. With a cold sweat moistening his palms and hot, live fire hovering above his head, he decided to give one last tug at the aronai with all the might remaining in him. The muscles in his stomach tightened and a deep, long grunt escaped through his clenched teeth as he wrapped the aronai a couple of times around his wrist and gave it a sudden jerk towards himself. And finally, it came off Birkhang's grip. Ojhai toppled over on his back and the free aronai slumped down in a mess on his face.

It took a while for Ojhai to take the aronai off his eyes and face because his hands were trembling; he was also trying to get back on his feet at the same time but realized that his legs were trembling too. With much effort and scuffle between him and the aronai when he at last got back on his feet and the aronai was off his face, he saw that Birkhang had removed his sandals, tucked them into the dhoti at his waist and was all set to break into a run. Only, his legs wouldn't move. They were numb with fright. The haraibankhas were still bouncing in the air above them. Ojhai picked up Birkhang's aronai and more out of habit than out of the sensible thinking of a mind that had stopped working since the tug of war, he wrapped it around his own head. He too removed his sandals and, taking them in one hand, nudged Birkhang hard with the other. And the men started to run as fast as their aged feet and heavy, well-fed bellies could carry them. The agitated haraibankhas gave chase, not to Birkhang but to the aronai that had whacked down on them again and again till a while ago. But now with that aronai on Ojhai's head, they were after Ojhai.

Around half a dozen haraibankhas sped along with Birkhang and Ojhai, above their heads, as they ran through the night across the field. Sometimes a couple of haraibankhas darted ahead to reach a tree some distance away and disappeared there. But they would abruptly reappear right in front of the fleeing men, sending them scurrying backwards. The way home seemed to have stretched into endlessness.

Now there was this one thing about Ojhai. The way others in his village took to prayers when they were in jubilation or a calamity, in sickness or good health, in terror or faith, Ojhai took to his siphoong. And now was one of those times. Out of sheer terror, while Birkhang began to cry, 'Jai Bathou Bwrai! Jai Bathou Bwrai!' Ojhai's trembling hands reached down to his waist and brought out the siphoong from where it was tucked into his own aronai. He didn't know what tune he would play. He just raised it to his lips. Birkhang was too engrossed in making his wobbly legs run to stop Ojhai from playing his siphoong. Even otherwise, now that the haraibankhas were chasing them, it didn't matter anymore to Birkhang whether Ojhai played his siphoong or desisted from doing so. So he just as well might, if it in anyway calmed Ojhai's own frayed nerves. And he did.

Ojhai began playing his siphoong.

Note after note, as his trembling fingers moved from one hole to another on the flute, the air around gradually seemed to get easier to breathe. He could once more feel, slowly but steadily, the ground returning beneath his bare feet. The cicadas and bush crickets fell silent to listen to Ojhai's siphoong. He was also slowly realizing what he was playing. In his tune was the sensuousness of the dark night and the yearning of lovers lost in that darkness. There was the cajoling of a mother putting her infant to sleep and so was the faith of the farmer begging for rains. The night too stopped in its tracks to listen to Ojhai. Birkhang cried no more. Though he continued to chant under his breath, 'Jai Bathou Bwrai!'

it was now no more out of sheer terror. It was instead with calmness and faith. He even mustered the courage to raise his head to look at the haraibankhas.

'Ojhai! My friend!' he whispered in awe. 'Don't stop! Continue playing. Carry on! Carry on!'

Ojhai carried on.

Birkhang asked Ojhai to carry on playing because he saw that even the haraibankhas had calmed down. They were no more restless and vengeful. The flicker in them softened to gentle wave-like movements from the jerking, panting animosity of a while ago. They now moved along with the men as if to listen to the siphoong and not to chase and scare. Ojhai and Birkhang realized that they had stopped running around frantically and their feet were now falling in steady steps on the right track, homewards.

Soon, one haraibankha came very close to another and gave itself up into its bosom. Two became one. Birkhang glanced at Ojhai. Ojhai nodded even as he continued to play, and an unspoken conversation transpired between the men. As they walked on, more haraibankhas merged themselves with others and soon they became much fewer in number too. However, they continued to follow the men. Hence, the men decided through nods and glances that they would not walk right into their village, to avoid leading the haraibankhas in with them. For who knew, they were spirits, after all. If they felt provoked or angered by someone or something again, they were totally capable of unleashing pandemonium upon the village. So, though they pretended to walk home, in reality, they were slowly and cleverly walking away from it.

As the men led the haraibankhas away from their village, a familiar tune from long ago suddenly flashed through Ojhai's mind. It was the same tune that he often used to play as a youth to herd the cattle back home at dusk. Ojhai even thought he heard, somewhere in the back of his mind, the clong-clang of copper bells around the neck of their cows. He started playing that tune. Shadows and silhouettes in the dark no more took Birkhang's breath away. The men walked past the row of tall trees that lined Braujen's fields and at the end of it, took a turn and started walking back towards where the first haraibankha appeared and joined them. Subdued and obedient, the few that remained followed, as if in a trance. Birkhang put his feet back into his sandals and quietly, without disturbing the flow of the music, took out Ojhai's sandals from where they were tucked into his dhoti's hold and gently placed them on the ground in front of his feet. Ojhai slipped into them without breaking the rhythm of their walk. He remembered, as he played the siphoong, how he used to herd the cattle back home in those olden days, and how his father would wait at the gate to help him put the cows into the shed, with the calves close to their mothers. He played on, as he remembered how his mother used to wait for him in the kitchen with roasted sweet potatoes or boiled tapioca. 'Thasumli roonanwi dwnbai,' she would call out, 'I have boiled some tapioca. Go wash your hands and feet before eating!' He remembered the lullabies she sang to him—tunes he often played on his siphoong. But now he played the cowherd's tune, herding the haraibankhas back to where they emerged from. And like the cattle, the haraibankhas followed. Ojhai looked up at them and wondered if they might be the spirits of his mother. And his father. And the last traces of fear fizzled away from his heart. He looked at the path ahead. The abode of the haraibankhas wasn't too far.

As they left the row of trees and started walking through the open fields, the fireflies reappeared. First one, then a few, then many more. They too began to follow Ojhai and Birkhang, flying above their heads, beside the haraibankhas. By the time they arrived at the spot where the first lone haraibankha had appeared earlier during the night, once again, only that lone haraibankha remained. The rest had all merged into it. Ojhai and Birkhang stopped. Ojhai continued to play his siphoong. Birkhang noticed that the tune had smoothly changed to that of a bride's send-off. There was sorrow in the tune at the parting of the bride, yet no desire to see her stay back. She had to leave. For her place was there where she was going. The situation was the same for the haraibankha. It had to leave and not stay back with the men. Ojhai stood there and continued playing. The men didn't know if it was an illusion, but the haraibankha seemed to grow smaller and become tamed as it circled above them and abruptly darted towards the top of a tree and disappeared. Ojhai and Birkhang remained standing there for a while, but no more haraibankhas appeared.

Birkhang reached out to Ojhai's head and slowly untying his aronai, wrapped it around his own neck. The aronai was his, after all. In doing so, as the free end of the aronai swung through the night, tiny flickers appeared. But this time, they were fireflies. They led the men on through the night once more, as if showing them their way home. An owl hooted. Birkhang smiled, loving the presence of life in the dark. He placed an arm across Ojhai's shoulder and said, 'Don't stop, Ojhai, play on! Keep playing on your siphoong!'

And Ojhai played on his siphoong till they reached their village and walked into their houses. There was some more of the night left for them to catch a few winks of sleep.

# Chapter 4

# FLAME

The waterfront by the beel at Madlagami that winter morning was bubbling with excitement!

Fun and frolic swept through the waters of the beel and the fields around it despite the chill in the air and grey clouds in the sky above. At least one member from every household had gathered there with fishing nets, fishing polo, khobai, jekai ... any fishing equipment that they could get their hands on, to participate in the community fishing in the shallow, waist-deep waters of the beel. Men pulled the front edge of their phali back between their legs and all the way up to their waist to tuck it there so that wading through the hyacinth was less messy. Older women folded up their dokhonas high up to their thighs, while a few younger ones lifted them up to their shins. They all were in the water, catching fish for the community feast later that evening. For it was the eve of Magw Domasi, the harvest festival. The village folks had toiled hard through the cultivation and the harvesting, and spent anxious nights for fear of losing their crops to dry spells, floods, bugs, birds and disease. But the crops were bountiful and their granaries were full. So now everyone was ready to celebrate the abundance.

The cloudy weather could in no way dampen the spirit of the villagers. There was much singing and cheering, and some discreet, light-hearted flirting and banter too. Some tied the khobai, the small wicker pitcher, to their waist and scooped into the water with the jekai. Others left their khobais on the banks, within reaching distance of the arm. So whatever fish, snail and crab came up in the jekai was transferred into the khobai. Some used small plastic or iron buckets instead of the khobai. Later, they would separate and sort out the catch, but for now, they put everything in together. Some moved among the merry crowd raising their fishing polo, and wherever they saw fish jumping about just underneath the surface of the water in the muddy beel, there they swung the polo down, splashing it into the waters to catch the fish. Yet others used large nets hanging from the ends of an x-shaped bamboo glider. They fished more towards the middle of the beel, where the water was deeper. They would lower it into the water, hold it down a while and raise it. These nets mostly caught fish which were slightly bigger. Sometimes even water snakes came up. When such slithering catch was caught, the air would fill with shrieks and shrill laughter, leading to much teasing.

Ojhai too had arrived at the waterfront early that morning along with his son. His daughter-in-law, like many other womenfolk, stayed home to prepare laru, sithau and other delicacies. These were mostly prepared using rice, with some dishes being sweet and some savoury. Today, he carried with him one of his long siphoongs, for it was a festive occasion. When Ojhai arrived, Birkhang and Daimalu were already there. Daimalu's head was cosily ensconced in the warmth of his faithful monkey cap with only the eyes and the little round nose peeking out. But in the chill of the morning, he forgot his jotha back at home.

Meanwhile, people had already started flocking and stepping into the cold water that numbed the feet. Despite the numbness on their feet, there was no stopping to their enthusiasm and they continued to spill into the beel.

'Never mind the chill!' old Mohan shouted when women squealed as they planted their feet in. 'Your feet will get used to it in a while. Go on, get hold of the big ones in there. Go on! In the name of Magw Domasi!' Saying this, he spun himself around in a merry jig. Mohan had already taken his morning swig of jou to warm his old bones. He arrived with neither woollens nor footwear, so warm had the jou rendered his nerves. As the villagers began to step into the shallow water, swarms of dragon flies rose from the water grass. Their paper-thin wings buzzed above the merry heads of the people, as if lending background music to Mohan's song.

*Gandoula Gandoula,*
*Dragonfly dragonfly,*
*Trap it not, let it lie.*
*Instead, let's partake,*
*Magw Domasi's savouries and cake!*
*Come, let's partake,*
*Let's relish and partake.*
*Let the dragonfly lie.*

By then, Ojhai had also arrived. 'There comes Abou Siphoong!' someone cried joyously. 'Blow into your siphoong, Abou, warm us up! Or else there'll be no fish for the feast tonight.'

'Here I go, then!' Ojhai shouted back. 'Get them khobais ready for some delicious catch!' Swaying and tapping his feet, he began to blow into his siphoong. Birkhang struck his kham and it roared to life. Daimalu clapped his hands in rhythm to Birkhang's kham and began singing:

*The water is cold, hei Jarou!*
*The water is cold,*
*Don't lift your dokhona so high.*
*Fish and crab,*
*We shall grab,*
*And fill your empty khobai!*

As the song rang above the waters, more people from there joined Daimalu while still at their fishing.

*The hyacinth we shall shove aside,*
*If we can't, may woe betide.*
*Dipping the polo, dipping the jekai,*
*We shall surely fill your khobai.*
*Jarou, keep ready the salt and chilli,*
*Joubidei and omakhasi.*
*We'll fill your khobai with snail, phithikhri,*
*For the feast of Magw Domasi!*

The merry fishing crowd hooted and cheered as they churned and waded through the waters of the beel, splashing others with mud and water, and soaking their bodies with the raw smell of fresh, live fish. That, however, only doubled the people's gusto. A few scanty drops of rain fell in between but went mostly unnoticed because the splash above the beel was far greater than the raindrops. Strains from Ojhai's long siphoong serenaded the people, bestowing their limbs with unprecedented vigour and agility to ensure a good catch. The music also dived into the waters and made the fish sashay into the polos and jekais. Just watching Ojhai immerse himself into his siphoong was so intensely gratifying that even without the jou, the senses began to get tipsy and wooed. He didn't know any scale or chord, raga or pitch, for he never learnt to play it professionally. He just learned to play it passionately.

While one group of villagers was catching fish, another group of young men was already out in the fields near the primary school. They had levelled out a stretch of the ground, breaking down clumps of earth and cutting down foot-long stalks of harvested paddy, preparing the place for the evening's feast. There they had erected a makeshift shed of bamboo and straw for the elderly to sit in. The young boys had also collected firewood and piled them on one side for the cooking. They had gone to the town of Gossaigaon the previous day and brought, on hire, large utensils to cook in. After the feast, most of the youth stayed back to spend the night by the fire, singing and dancing. Then, early the next morning, they would set fire to the shed.

That year, Madlagami had a good harvest and so the Magw Domasi was a joyous one. Two fat pigs were slaughtered and a part of the meat was being smoked. The sweet jou too had already been brewed in most homes. Ojhai's daughter-in-law had also brewed three pots full. Hers was really sweet. How Ojhai, Daimalu and Birkhang loved it! But for now, Ojhai was lost in his siphoong, whistling notes of joy to the exhilarating rhythm of Birkhang's kham. Their music spurred the villagers on. Even the gathering grey clouds failed to hold them back. Ojhai got so carried away that, as he played, he danced closer and closer to the crowd and to the water. When he paused for breath, he shouted with glee in a sing song tone, 'Hoi, lwgwfwr! Hoi, friends! Here I come with more melody, keep your khobais ready, for some real good catch!' Saying so, as he resumed playing and dancing, someone's khobai indeed got a good and rare catch: Ojhai's foot!

So engrossed was Ojhai in his tune that he missed seeing the wicker pitcher, and as he stepped on it, slippery as its mouth was with mud and water, his foot easily slid in past the narrow neck and landed inside the big, round belly of the khobai. Ojhai would have still limped and danced on imagining it to be a fishing boot, had it not been for the occupants in there. He suddenly paused and even as he stared at Daimalu, he was actually sensing his foot in the khobai and then abruptly let out a massive, ear-splitting shriek. It rang through the crowd, making everyone turn towards the yell. When the long shriek ended for lack of breath, Ojhai took a deep one and once more started a new shriek. When that ended, another one came up, then another and yet another, each in varying pitch and tune, length and strength. And all this while, poor Ojhai was sometimes standing and sometimes hopping on the khobai-less foot, trying with all his limb and lung power to kick the khobai off the other foot. Sometimes he flayed his arms in pain, though still holding on to his siphoong and sometimes looped them under the thigh with the khobai to support its muscles because they were beginning to pull and stretch from being lifted for so long. But whatever he did with his limbs, his wails never ceased.

'He must have broken a bone in there!' old Mohan wondered aloud.

'No, maybe he grazed the skin,' someone else contested.

'Dheii, you dimwits,' said Khobin, 'a nail or a couple of them must have turned all the way around in his toes! Those hurt worse than a broken bone, you see, I had one catching turtles once. And such hideous pain there—'

'You stop with your story now, old man!' his wife snapped. Then she looked at Daimalu and said, 'Do you think a toe might have come off from the rest of the foot?' She didn't wait for an answer, though.

Through all this speculation, no one heard what Ojhai was trying to say between his shrieks and yelps all this while. Birkhang and Daimalu were doing their best to help. Birkhang knelt down and made Ojhai rest the calf of his victimized leg on his shoulder, while Daimalu began pulling the khobai from the other end.

'Isn't it amazing, huh,' Nobin remarked, 'that slipping in there was such a smooth sail but slipping out now is such a constipation.' And the fellow burst out into a guffaw, only to be silenced curtly by Toroni. Nobin had been living off only jou since his fields had been harvested. That day, people could smell him from a mile away, despite the pervading stench of raw fish by the beel.

'Poor guy is in excroooociating pain and you guffaw, what? Have some shame, Nobin!' Toroni reprimanded him. 'Have some compassion as well. Could be your foot next time!' Saying this, Toroni only gently shoved him away from Ojhai, but the fellow plonked to the ground and never got up till the time the fishing went on. The crowd buzzed in solidarity with Ojhai and nodded in agreement with Toroni.

Birkhang continued to tug and pull to the sound of aquatic life doing a roller-coaster act around the foot inside the khobai. Fishing at the beel came to a pause. Ojhai continued to shriek. The tip of his nose and his ears had become red and his forehead was beginning to glisten with sweat even on that chill, cloudy winter's morning.

'Pinching! Pinching!' Ojhai screamed.

Onlookers looked at one another, shook their heads and sympathized with poor Ojhai. 'Loose ends of cane. Yeah, that's what is pinching,' they concluded.

And then, just when poor Ojhai was shouting, 'Biting, aiyaahh! Biting! Aideelei, aidee!' Suddenly, with one great yank, Daimalu managed to get the khobai off his foot. The abrupt release made Daimalu fall on his back on the swampy ground with the errant khobai emptying its contents of small fish over whatever of his face was peeking out of his monkey cap and into the insides of his sweater. But Ojhai continued to shout. And then he realized that a collective shriek louder than his own was filling the waterfront. When he shut his mouth to look at the crowd, he saw that they were staring, pointing and shaking their jekais at his injured foot. So Ojhai too looked down at it. And what he saw down there yielded another great yell. A crab almost the size of his big toe was holding on to it with its pincers! How much ever Ojhai shook his foot, it refused to let go. Someone ran to look for a big leaf to grab the crab and detach it. Meanwhile, old Rongjalee doubled a side of her dokhona and, holding the crab with it, gave it a good jerk, pulled it off and hurled it away. Ojhai let out one last, enormous scream and in his agony, let the siphoong slip into the mud.

'You'll be fine, Ojhai! You'll be alright!' Khobin pacified him. 'Oi! Help him to that mound and let him sit awhile!'

And so Ojhai was helped to the small mound a few steps away and made to sit a while till his foot felt well enough to take him home. A little girl picked up the siphoong, wiped off the mud with her skirt, and brought it with reverence to Ojhai. One by one, the people once more waded back into the water; but now they had to do without the cheering spirit of the siphoong. When Ojhai felt he was ready to walk back home, Daimalu and Birkhang helped him up, took an arm each around their shoulders, tucked the siphoong into the aronai at Ojhai's waist, and left for his home.

'Don't worry, folks!' Ojhai shouted back over his shoulder, not letting a crab pinch the festive spirit away from his heart. 'I'll be back for the feast later in the evening. Save my share of the fish and jou!'

'Done, Abou! Done!' Dhanonjoy shouted back dotingly.

'Mine too.' Daimalu waved back.

'Make mine double of theirs!' Birkhang yelled joyously.

'For sure, Abou!' Dhanonjoy laughed.

Restoring mirth and enthusiasm back among the fishing villagers who braved the dreary weather for the night's feast, the three limped away.

All through the rest of the morning, the villagers continued with their fishing. Along with fish and snails, crabs too came up in their nets, jekais and polos. After hours of random catching, the men sat down to sort out the assortment. They put away the large rohu and ari fish aside to go into a curry of tomatoes. The very small, finger-sized fish and those even smaller, would be thrown into a gravy of green herbs. The catfish and spotted snakehead would be barbequed in the bonfire and then eaten with salt and green chilli. These, however, would begin to be served well ahead of the main meal, as accompaniment to pots and pots of jou while the feast would be cooked. And by the time the meal was ready, these accompaniments would all be devoured. The crabs too would be roasted, to be carefully shelled and made into a chutney. The snails, of course, would go into a curry of black gram with kharei. Not to forget the two fat pigs. Back at home, visualizing all of the steaming delicacies was stimulation enough for Ojhai to forget the pain in the pinched toe and to look forward to being a part of the sumptuous Magw Domasi feast in the evening.

So, come evening, Ojhai, Daimalu and Birkhang were back at the feast grounds. The oldest of the old at Madlagami too turned up for the feast, even if it required them to be bundled up in all the woollens they owned. Ojhai came limping with the same long siphoong that he had carried to the waterfront in the morning. Birkhang had the kham's cloth belt slung across his shoulder, while the kham itself hung at his rear like a bag. Daimalu too brought his jotha along this time, for there would be much more dancing and merry-making by the bonfire than there had been in the morning by the beel. Besides Ojhai's enthralling tunes, there would be the happy indulgence of the sweet jou to lift their spirits and revel in the festive cheer. However, Ojhai regretted that he would not be able to dance.

'But at least you're able to come and be a part of the merry feast, Ojhai. Be grateful to providence!' Birkhang scolded him in mock anger.

'Isn't our Ojhai one greedy pig?' Daimalu laughed.

A few women were peeling heaps of potato and some were peeling onions, wiping away tears and drawing in the snot that the onion induced. Some were chopping brinjals and pumpkin for the labra. Some were grinding ginger, garlic and chilli in small mortars using pestles. The fish and snail had already been cleaned.

'Oi, Abou! Come on, start your siphoong,' a young boy called out. 'Only then will we be able to cut the pork into pieces of the right size!'

'Come then, Ojhai, Daimalu,' Birkhang said, pulling the kham to the front and hitting it off.

Daimalu too stood up and, clapping his jotha, began his verse:

*If you're done with the laru and sithau,*
*O pretty agei Jarou,*
*Come serve the oma, serve the jou,*
*While the fire's still aglow.*
*Janwsei lwngnwsei magw domasi*
*Let's get into a feasting spree!*

Ojhai remained sitting as he brought the siphoong passionately to his lips, as if it were the lips of his beloved and not merely a piece of bamboo pipe with holes. But then, his bond with his siphoong had always been so much more than that of a musical instrument and its player. It was like the relationship between breath and soul. However, when he blew into it now, no music played. Never in all his more than sixty winters had such a thing occurred! Stunned, he brought it down, shook it hard, and once more took it to his lips. No, nothing happened. It was as if the air didn't pass through the flute; as if his own breath was getting choked. When he looked through the mouth end of the siphoong, he realized that something was lodged in it.

'Now, now, what might that be?' Ojhai spoke to himself. 'Would someone please care to fetch a twig for me?' he asked of no one in particular.

Little children scurried to be the first to reach Abou Siphoong with a twig. And when the twig arrived, he poked it into the siphoong and felt something slightly hard, slightly crusty inside. It moved on its own too. Suddenly, the leg of a creature appeared through one of the holes.

'It's a crab's limb!' Daimalu shouted, standing next to Ojhai.

It was the same crab that had pinched Ojhai's big toe in the morning. When Rongjalee grabbed the crab and hurled it to the ground, it was so confused and terrified that the insides of the siphoong, which too had slipped from Ojhai's hands by then, was the nearest safe crevice it could find. So it crawled and lodged itself there. It had since hiked a ride in the siphoong to Ojhai's home and back and was now once more amidst the same merry crowd. Ojhai shook the siphoong, blew hard into it and even tried pushing the crab out the other end with the twig, but the obstinate creature clung on to the siphoong like it had to Ojhai's toe earlier, having a convenient grip in the hole with a limb.

'Blow harder, Abou. Play a tune of marching soldiers,' a little boy suggested. 'Only then will the crab march out feeling heroic about going into battle.'

'Uff, son!' Ojhai laughed. 'But with your soldier blocking this bugle, how can I play a marching song?'

The people standing around and watching the drama nodded.

Ojhai blew and blew into the siphoong but could neither blow out the crab nor create any music. A little distance away, those preparing to cook blew and blew into the firewood but could not build a fire because the firewood had become damp from the morning's drizzle. Those in charge of cooking threw in many a matchstick into the wood and blew into it with bamboo pipes and pipes of iron, but the kindling only emitted thick swirls of smoke that made people cough and squint. Jwngsaar fanned the firewood with the large round lid of a cooking vessel. Yet no flame appeared.

'Pour some more kerosene in there, boys!' Langthee shouted as she mixed salt and turmeric powder into the pieces of fish.

'Then light five matchsticks together, drop all of them into the firewood and voila! Watch the flames rise!'

The young boys did just as she told them to. The flames did rise, but never really clawed into the wood. As soon as they had licked up all the kerosene fed to them, they sunk back and fizzled away. Smoke bellowed once more. While the evening grew darker and colder, neither the firewood nor Ojhai's siphoong got started. The old were beginning to get restless, children were beginning to yawn, and the young people who had organized the whole feast were getting nervous.

'If only Ojhai and his siphoong could coax and plead with the firewood to light up,' an exasperated young woman sighed.

'I wish we could, young lady,' Ojhai said thoughtfully, 'but the siphoong's caught a crab and its nostril is blocked. However, let me try once more, since you request so endearingly.' And he took his lute once more to his mouth—not sideways as if to blow gently to create music, but straight and with the whole mouth of the siphoong shoved into his own, as if it were a leg of chicken. Meanwhile, Rongjalee chose that exact moment to come up to the siphoong and stick up an eye into the other hole to see how far up the crab was holed in. Now Ojhai had already heaved in a long haul of breath, filled in his lung and with great momentum, sent the entire lungful of air sweeping down the siphoong like a hurricane. The force of the air managed to get the crab to detach its limb from the hole of the siphoong and sent it hurtling like a meteor right into Rongjalee's eye.

'Wha … a … aa, aiyou lei hobab!' She screamed and frantically beat her palms across her face to push away the crab. In that little acrobatic feat, her shawl fell off her chest and the crab landed right into her bosom. Scared, confused and once more seeking dark crevices, it began crawling further down. Even before Ojhai's head could think, his hand instinctively raised the siphoong and, jabbing the little creature with its tip, slashed through Rongjalee's panting bosom over her dokhona, brushing away the crab with it as it went. The poor creature fell to the ground and scurried away sideways, looking for a new hideout while a collective squeal rose from the feasters. At last, Ojhai's siphoong was cleared.

However, the fire for cooking was yet to get started because most of the people had come away from the makeshift kitchen to de-crab Ojhai's siphoong. But now that it was breathing free, Dhanonjoy said, 'Ei, Abou, come blow into the cooking fire with your magic wand. Command it with your melody to light up. Or else we'll end up eating only smoke for this year's Magw Domasi. Come on, Abou!'

'I surely would, dear boy, but doesn't my siphoong have holes all along it? The air I blow won't even reach down to those arrogant firewood brats.'

'Oh ho! Hear, hear, good folks!' Birkhang bantered. 'The wind Ojhai passes will go in vain!' He roared with such a resounding laughter, making gestures of passing wind, that it rolled amidst the crowd, infecting everyone it grazed.

'Never mind all that, Abou,' Jwngsaar insisted. 'Come, please give it a try.'

Ojhai knew it would be a futile effort. Yet, he didn't have the heart to refuse these young boys who had been so enthusiastically planning for days to make the feast a memorable one for the entire village. He realized they were now beginning to feel lost.

'Righto, then, fellow feasters!' said Ojhai, putting up a cheerful front and hobbling towards the cooking fire. 'Give way to one limping old man and a holed blow-pipe!'

'Wahaiyaah! Give way!' repeated Birkhang, letting his kham roar up a war beat as he cautiously walked alongside Ojhai.

Near the fire, Ojhai knelt down and, from a safe distance, blew into it. The free-flowing wind in it instinctively brought Ojhai's fingers to tap rhythmically over the holes, creating music that came to him not from planning but from absolute passion. The music slowly spread over the damp firewood, then floated out among the feasting villagers and into the harvested fields and winter skies of Madlagami. Even the night paused to listen. Night birds and insects hushed themselves to listen to the siphoong. Those gathered at the feast had always been hearing the strains of Ojhai's siphoong and were fondly familiar with them. And yet, each time they heard those strains, they were mesmerized all over again, as if it was the first time they were hearing them. It was the same that day at the feast. All of a sudden, everything and everyone became still and quiet—enthralled, in a trance. Even Birkhang and Daimalu stood still and stared into the fire, their kham and jotha silent. Only Ojhai's flute rang into the night, blowing into the damp firewood. There was no song, no dance. Not then. This kind of passionate effort often left Ojhai breathless, for it was a matter of the trust the people he loved placed in him. While Ojhai's siphoong cajoled and commanded, threatened and wooed the firewood to light up, all else was paralysed and all eyes stared into the firewood, as if waiting for some magic to happen.

And it did!

'Flame!' a little girl gasped, pointing at the fire. 'Look, Ayei, flame!' She showed her mother. The delight in her tender eyes spoke of the unanimous delight of all the people gathered there. And indeed, there was a tiny tongue of flame at the base of the thick, evil smoke. It appeared like hope amidst gloom, like strength against evil, like a power that could protect the villagers and bless their fields with bounty.

'Yes, Ayei, it is a flame!' she repeated, jumping with joy. Her mother hugged her in response.

'Hurrah, Abou!' The gathering suddenly went wild with joy and relief.

'Jai Bathou Bwrai!' they shouted their gratitude. 'Jai Magw Domasi!' they cheered.

Birkhang's hands began falling rapidly once more at his kham, its pace and rhythm going faster along with the tapping of his feet. Daimalu's jotha too came back to life.

'Keep going, Abou Siphoong! Keep going!' Dhanonjoy pleaded as he hurried people to place the pots and pans on the fire to start the cooking. Young people began singing and dancing, and a flurry of cooking activities began immediately. With his faith renewed and his confidence oozing, Ojhai closed his eyes and let his soul take over the whistling of the siphoong. The flame rose and rose until it took into its embrace all the firewood near it and sucked up all the dampness from them. Someone brought Ojhai a khamplai to sit comfortably near the fire, stretching out the leg with the pinched toe, so that he could continue with his enthralling music. As the flame rose, so did the smoke fall, till it sank into the ashes. And so did the fire for the feast of Magw Domasi start. Lasit fed more firewood into the fire and, despite the dampness, the fresh logs too were promptly sucked into the flames. The blaze continued to glow with zeal through the entire process of cooking of all the varied curries of fish, snail and meat. Even after the cooking got over, the cooks kept feeding firewood to the fire, a little at a time, to keep the fire going. Its glow watched over Madlagami's fields all through that night of Magw Domasi. Such was the magic of the music Ojhai and his siphoong created.

'Now then, lwgwfwr,' Rongjalee announced. 'Let us begin with the feast. Let the joubidei flow!' and sat down on the edge of a bedcover spread over a layer of dry, warm thatch. More such bundles of thatch were strewn about for people to sit on. Some had bedsheets spread on them, but most were left just as they were. Children rolled and tumbled on them, getting straw all over their hair and sweaters, making gleeful messes of themselves. The soft, combined radiance of the firewood and the kerosene lanterns on the faces of the people only made them look all the merrier. As if the play of light and darkness was teasing the senses of the revellers who were likewise a little aware, a little tipsy.

However, no sooner had Rongjalee sat down than she jumped up, letting out a terrible yelp and beating her rear. Langthee, who was sitting next to her, narrowed her eyes and focussed her sight on Rongjalee's hand movements. The poor vision of her aged eyes conspired with the dark to make her see nothing much at first. So she brought her eyes close—very close—to Rongjalee's rear and then she too let out a yelp.

'Aiyaah! Crab! Crab!'

Now Langthee's yelp emerged only because it shocked her to find a crab at such an unexpected and untoward place during such an unanticipated hour. Otherwise, she wasn't one to be spooked by crabs and snakes. The crab held fast to Rongjalee's dokhna at the back and refused to let go. It was, however, the thickness of the fabric that saved the evening for her. Langthee being the daring woman that she was, who wouldn't be bothered by pinches and bites, and also because she knew how to catch a creature with pincers, pulled at the crab with her thick-skinned bare hands, brought it near the cooking fire and took a good look at it.

'Now what say, Rongjalee? Come, take a look,' she called her friend.

Still rubbing her rear, Rongjalee walked up to the fire to take a good look at the crab. 'Why now, I swear! Look, Ojhai,' she said excitedly. 'It's the same crab!'

Ojhai stepped closer to the fire and, bending over the creature, looked hard at it. 'Nwngou! Nwngou! Yeah, for sure it is!' he said with rapid nods of his slightly tipsy head.

'Pray, why is it after us, eh, my merciful Bathou? Who knows who it is going to pinch next!' Daimalu exclaimed.

'That so, huh?' Langthee looked at Rongjalee and then at the crab in her palm. 'In which case, does anyone know what to do with it?'

Just as they were wondering what to do with the crab, and when everyone was silently and mentally beginning to feel all over themselves sensations of pinches and stings, the crab, as before, began looking for a dark crevice to hide in. But this time it couldn't crawl far. Exhausted and injured from much spinning, poking and blowing since morning, it fell from Langthee's palm and rolled away into the fire. In its final moment, the fire pinched out its pincers and lapped out its life.

'Uh oh!' Ojhai murmured, almost pitying the crab's end. 'The flames knew what to do with it.'

'But, hey! I too know what to do with it,' Langthee exclaimed as a sudden brainwave swept over her. 'To not let such a good crab go to waste. Bring on the music, you old men!'

So while Ojhai, Daimalu and Birkhang resumed their music and the rest of the people stirred and spiced the meat in the cooking pot and watched Langthee. She dragged the crab out of the fire, pulled off its limbs and placed it back on the embers for just a while longer. Meanwhile, she took a few swigs of jou and did a few spins of dance to the music of the three old men. Barbequed and salted snakehead and catfish were doing the rounds between whistles and song. The music of the siphoong soared. And when Langthee felt the crab was roasted well, she took it out of the embers, dipped it in water to cool it and then neatly shelled it. Only an adept hand could do the shelling the way her fingers did the job. When she was done, she sprinkled some salt on it and brought it to Ojhai.

'Nei, old man!' she said with adoration in her eyes but banter in her voice. 'The tale of the crab started with you. Let it end with you too. Here, for starters with your jou. Oi there, child,' she called out randomly to a group of children playing about in the straw, 'get a nice, fiery, green chilli for our old man here, our siphoong master, to burn down that crab in his guts so that its ghost doesn't pinch him further down!' Saying so, she let forth an infectious guffaw that rolled through the Domasi revellers, leaving them all in splits.

Even as a biting chill descended upon the harvested fields and a thick fog rose above the beel, there was warmth in the hearts of the villagers and there was Ojhai's music to make those hearts dance. Their granaries were well stocked. The aroma of a whole lot of delicacies filled the night air, setting their stomachs rumbling and their tongues drooling. Ojhai's siphoong was once more free, breathing and filled with lively notes that kept the cooking flames glowing! It was blissful.

# Chapter 5

# SONG OF SPRING

Bwisagu was just round the corner.

But spring that year was a parched, dreary and reclusive one in the village of Madlagami. The rains had not yet arrived. What arrived elsewhere in the country, instead, was an all-encompassing, unheard of disease from a land thousands of miles away, from across the mountains. One after another, it maimed and crippled nations, leaving millions dead and many more sick and gasping for breath in its trail. Health workers, volunteers and police went from village to village around Madlagami asking people to stay in their own homes and yards. And if at all they had to go to buy stuff like salt and mustard oil or kerosene oil, they asked the villagers not to get too close to others. They also gave people tiny pieces of garments with ear-bands to wear over their mouths and noses. Masks, they called those.

'This way,' they told the village folks, 'you'll keep the disease from catching you, from entering your bodies and from ravaging Madlagami.'

'But what strange disease is this that we have to hide from, covering part of our faces like robbers?' Ojhai had asked them when they visited his homestead.

'The name is actually a simple one, Abou, and a pretty one too. It's called Corona.'

'Eh,' Ojhai smiled, 'doesn't sound dangerous, does she?'

'So do most pretty things, Abou,' the health worker winked, 'but they are! Never mind that. Just stay to yourself, till we tell you when it's alright to be out there with your friends again.'

How Ojhai longed to walk around to see and feel the bewitching spring in his village!

Alone and by himself in his own courtyard, Ojhai would sometimes whistle into his siphoong and at other times listen to the cuckoo, the black drongo and the keteki singing spring songs. And when he played these in his siphoong, the birds flew down from their perch on his thatched roof and cocked their heads to look at the flute, wondering what kind of featherless bird it was. Or so Ojhai interpreted. But sometimes they remained on the thatch till they were done with their little mating ritual. Ojhai's homestead was like most other Bodo homesteads in Madlagami, with the kitchen towards the east and the rest of the house made into individual hutments and placed around the courtyard. The Sijou plant was always planted in the north-east corner of the courtyard. The approach to his courtyard was at the south, and a little into the courtyard from the approach road was the large, wide-canopied gulmohar tree under which his son had fashioned a bench out of unsplit bamboo for Ojhai to sit during summer afternoons and evenings, and play his siphoong. And his daughter-in-law always kept the courtyard spic-and-span, sweeping away the tiny speckles of yellow leaves that kept falling from the gulmohar tree with even the gentlest whiff of breeze.

So, confined to his own home and yard in those days, it was on that bench that he spent most of his waking hours, sometimes even sitting quietly and listening to his daughter-in-law's spindle scurrying through the yarns in her loom as she sat weaving new gamosas and phalis for Bwisagu. Sometimes he cleaned the barn, sorting through old, unused objects that he hadn't thrown away thinking he just might need them someday. Up on the rafters in the barn, he found an old kham too. How he longed to hear the beats of Birkhang's kham!

But that year, Bwisagu would be a quiet one. The few thick and long, mauve foxtail orchids that clung to a branch of the gulmohar, tied there with a piece of rag, made a brave attempt to bloom and bring some solace to Ojhai. For days now, staying home all day and having nothing much to do, Ojhai even came to notice a pair of pigeons on his thatch. The male would puff up his chest feathers and go round and round crooning and gurgling *coo-croo-coo* to woo the female. Meanwhile, on the branches of the gulmohar, a spotted dove bobbed his head as he sought union with his mate. It filled Ojhai's heart to see so much love in his very own homestead. It made him think of his beloved wife, the way he used to play the siphoong for her around this time of the year, just when Bwisagu was about to arrive, and she would hum a song:

Porbatjhorayao
Dongphang dannw thang bla
Sal, gandwi, makhu angnw
Danna labw nanghwnai

*To Porbatjhoray when you go,*
*To gather wood,*
*Do fetch for me without fail,*
*Sal wood for my spindle!*

Ojhai would take the siphoong off his lips to sing:

*Gladly, I shall, my beloved, my precious,*
*I shall fetch wood for your spindle,*
*But you, my dear, keep ready,*
*Sweet wine for me!*

In all the past Bwisagus after she passed away, Ojhai did hear birdsong but never really listened to them. Now, though, he did. He noticed. And then he closed his eyes and let his siphoong reply.

It was during one of those lonely afternoons that Ojhai chanced upon the little santhal boy in the yard across his, just beyond the path. He had seen the boy earlier but never really noticed him. Till then, the boy had always been a mere passing figure in the background. Such a tiny, malnourished, dusty-limbed child he was, with curly hair that had turned brown—like dried stalks of jute—from having rarely been oiled or washed. But that day, when Ojhai sat facing Tara's yard, mending a goat breach in his own fence, he spotted the boy on the charpoy in the shade of the large elephant apple tree in the small, unfenced yard. He was lying on his stomach, his thin legs on the bare ropes of the charpoy and the upper part of his body hanging down as he patted the goat and kept rubbing his head against hers, while her kids suckled her from below. There was a brown dog too on the charpoy—asleep, with its head resting on the boy's feet. Ojhai forgot his work and watched the boy instead. There didn't seem to be anyone else at home. A few piglets lay close to one another at the foot of the elephant apple tree, on the other side of the charpoy. From where he was, Ojhai couldn't tell how many. A few hens clucked about in the yard, close to the little boy, pecking at ants on the dry, sun-baked ground. Ojhai stood up to see better. The house was a tiny, meagre shed with mud walls, no verandah and no electricity cable going in. One part of the roof comprised a rusty, storm-bent corrugated iron sheet and the other part was made of mould-ridden, sparse thatch. It surprised Ojhai that despite *seeing* this place everyday, he never *looked* at it, never noticed it at all. Until that moment.

When the boy rolled over and saw Ojhai gazing at him, he sat up and grinned. He wore only a strip of loin around his waist and a vest that seemed a size too large for him. It had holes in it. Ojhai grinned back. His heart went out to the boy.

'Had your meal, son?' Ojhai shouted across the narrow dirt road that separated the two yards. The only vehicle that went by that way once in a while was Mogen's bullock cart. Besides, of course, a few bicycles.

The boy shook his head.

'Not hungry?' Ojhai asked.

The little boy nodded. He was hungry.

Ojhai asked no further.

'I forget the name!' Ojhai shouted instead, after a while. 'What was it?'

The boy stood up on the charpoy and shouted, 'JUGNOO … OO … O!'

'Jugnu, eh?' Ojhai laughed.

The child nodded vigorously this time. Then he held up the dog, making him stand on his hind legs, and shouted once more, 'Batloo … oo!'

'Whoa! So that's Batloo, eh?' Jugnu's liveliness made the old man smile.

Jugnu nodded again, placing the dog down on all fours once more.

By now, Ojhai had resumed his work on the fence, but he kept talking to Jugnu. A while later, the boy went into the house and brought out a banana. He peeled it, ate some of it and shared the rest with the goat. She ate the peel too.

'And where's your mother?' Ojhai asked, not looking at the boy but hitting the head of a sliced length of bamboo with the wooden handle of his dao to push it into the hard ground, aligning it with the rest of the fence.

'Gone,' Jugnu shouted in reply, 'to bring rice. And potatoes, maybe.'

'Didn't you wish to go?' Ojhai asked, weaving in and out horizontally through the waist-high bamboo supports using a long length of a thin slice of bamboo.

The boy nodded, but Ojhai didn't see. His head was bent over the fence.

'Mai said it's far,' Jugnu replied, 'and that I'll get tired and will cry to be carried. And she will already have the bag of rice and stuff, so won't have her hands free to carry me too.' He went on to explain to Ojhai that last week too she had gone to Khiden's school to bring food.

Their conversation was a mix of Bodo and Santhali, which took Ojhai back to his own childhood. When he was a young boy and when the two people—the Bodos and Santhals—lived, played, ate, worked and celebrated Bwisagu side by side. Those days, Ojhai too used to speak Santhali as expertly as he spoke his own tongue. But today he found himself faltering. For since the Bodo–Santhal riots in the late 1990s, there had been a swift, sad drifting away of the two people. Ojhai felt sad because the riots, he heard, were instigated by those not from his land. Now as he remembered those times, his heart ached all over again. He had lost many of his friends in that mayhem, both Bodo and Santhal. Jugnu's grandfather Marcus was one among them. Now as the little boy spoke in fragmented Bodo and Santhali, Ojhai gathered that Tara had gone to collect relief food material that was being distributed by some private organization in the Laphakata Primary School.

'And who is Khiden? Your friend?' Ojhai asked.

'You don't know Khiden?' the little boy questioned in return. 'Why, Khiden, down by the broken wooden bridge. How he climbs trees! Atta boy! And he can hop the longest on one leg around here. Do you recognize him now?'

'Guess I do.' But Ojhai didn't, actually. 'So that is Khiden's school, eh?'

Jugnu nodded.

'And yours?'

'I don't go to school.'

Ojhai looked up now. The boy was big enough to go to school.

'Why so, Jugnu?'

Jugnu held the edge of the loin cloth he was wearing and flapped it ever so lightly as he said, 'I don't want to go to school in this. I'll go when Mai manages to get me a pair of pants. She said she will soon.'

Ojhai swallowed a lump in his throat.

The sun was high and it was past midday. Ojhai called his daughter-in-law and she put some puffed rice, jaggery, a few rice cakes laced with sesame, coconut and sugar, that she had prepared for Bwisagu, and two eggs in a paper bag and walked up to the fence. 'Nei, Gotho!' She waved at Jugnu. 'Come take this. Eat, okay?'

She smiled seeing the boy jump off the charpoy and come running towards her. She stretched her hand as far out to the other side of the fence as she could and held out the bag. The little boy took it and immediately inspected the contents, bringing the bag very close to his tiny head. It melted Ojhai's heart to see his face light up seeing the rice cakes. His eyes twinkled like fireflies. Jugnu. Maybe that's why Tara named him thus. Jugnu.

'Ask Tara to cook the eggs for you, alright?' Ojhai's daughter-in-law told him.

Jugnu nodded and grinned. An urge swept through her to rush to him and bring his entire little being into her embrace and hold him long and close to her bosom. But then she remembered what the health-workers had said: 'Keep safe distance from others.' She couldn't understand how loving a child could be hazardous to health. But she abided, nevertheless. Ojhai could see through her emotions. Jugnu had reached his yard and had taken out a rice cake. He joyously waved it at Ojhai in between eating it.

Ojhai had finished his work of mending the goat breach in the fence by then, but he just felt like hanging around there a while longer, till Jugnu finished his rice cake. So he sat down on a piece of thick unslit bamboo and brought out the siphoong from the tuck of the aronai at his waist. As Ojhai began blowing into it softly and slowly, a kind of soothing lethargy began to cascade out of his yard, across to Jugnu's and out into Madlagami's heat and dust. Gradually, the ferocity of the hot afternoon seemed to have mellowed to the notes of the siphoong. As Ojhai continued to play, gazing at Jugnu, the little boy slowly slid down on the charpoy and lay his head on Batloo's back, letting one arm hang down to feel the mother goat near him. He had licked up the last bits of the rice cake from his fingers. While he remained thus, Ojhai played on softly, lulling the child to sleep. Somewhere in the distant groves, a blue-throated barbet sang along to the notes of the siphoong, keeping pace and rhythm with the daughter-in-law's spindle diving through yarns in the loom, dragging with it more yarn in and out as she wove, just as Ojhai wove the bamboo fence. Even Batloo did not pull himself away from under Jugnu's sleeping head. The goat hunched on her knees and kept watch from under the charpoy. They all let the sleeping child be.

*No wonder*, Ojhai thought, *Tara didn't think she left her child home alone.* He brought the siphoong down but remained sitting there a while, keeping watch over the child. He waited till Tara appeared in the distance, balancing one sack on her head, a bag in the folds of an arm and a bottle in the other hand. She didn't look like she had managed a pair of pants for Jugnu yet. Her dark skin glistened with sweat as the late afternoon sun shone down on her face, making her squint. Her bare feet kicked up a thin trail of dust behind her, as thin as she herself was. She wore her saree like a skirt and topped it with a man's faded shirt. Maybe the saree wasn't of full length; maybe it was torn halfway, because of which she wrapped it the way she did. Or so Ojhai assumed.

As the sun began gliding down towards the western horizon, Ojhai got up and gathered his dao, wire and the bamboo shavings. The fact that it took a pandemic and extreme seclusion for him to take notice of this adorable little child and his weather-beaten young mother, in their yard that was filled with life yet was in dearth, made him pensive as he walked into the house.

Soon, it became routine for Ojhai and Jugnu to be in each other's company, each from his own yard. Sometimes the stillness of the afternoon would be punctuated only by Ojhai's daughter-in-law's spindle as it flew back and forth, as if looking for something. She was weaving phalis for her father-in-law, her husband and her brother-in-law. There was still no sign of rain, still no sign of the disease retreating. Ojhai would listen to the news in his little transistor, of how the pandemic preyed on more and more victims each day, ravaging nations. Ojhai missed Daimalu and Birkhang and their evening sessions of impromptu bagurumba in one or the other of their courtyards. He missed ushering in Bwisagu. On afternoons when he felt too low to even play his siphoong and just sat under the gulmohar, Jugnu would stand up on his charpoy and look out for him. When he saw Ojhai, he would shout out, 'Hoi siphoong! Not playing today?' The boy somehow always made Ojhai's spirits rise. He had so much life in him, so much to give, despite having so little. And Ojhai never had the heart to refuse him. So he would take the siphoong to his lips. The child would listen for a while as he played around in his yard with the goat kids and Batloo. Then, when he slowed down and came with the dog to sit on the charpoy, Ojhai knew it was time for him to switch the siphoong's tune over to a lullaby. And the child would gently drop his head on the dog and go off to sleep.

One afternoon, as Ojhai played the siphoong in his yard, Jugnu was playing in his own yard using tamarind seeds as marbles. It was then that they heard a keteki call from afar. Jugnu stopped his game, craned his neck to listen and quickly jumped up on the charpoy. He searched Ojhai out in his yard and, waving at him, shouted in glee, 'Laphasaiko, mophou bedor!'

Ojhai laughed heartily. For that's what the keteki said, in Bodo, through her song, it seemed: lapha greens and meat of the monitor lizard. The boy sang it with such happy abandon, in sync with the keteki, matching its tune and pitch, that it once again reminded Ojhai of his own childhood. While people all over the world were searching for ways to fight the pandemic and to deal with stress and trauma, Ojhai realized that he had a lot to search for and look at in his own backyard.

One afternoon, Ojhai looked for Jugnu in their yard, but couldn't spot the child. He walked closer to the fence and peered as far back into Jugnu's yard as his eyes could go. The lad was nowhere. When Ojhai didn't hear his voice either, his heart skipped a beat. Might the boy have taken ill? Could the disease they called corona have caught up? But he immediately cursed his mind for even letting such a thought cross it. He walked along the fence, straining his neck towards the yard across, beyond the path. Right then, from behind the little shed that the mother and son called home, the boy emerged, his tiny hand held lovingly by Tara. Relief swept through Ojhai. He realized how beautiful a bond had grown across the path between their two yards in these few days of seclusion, especially between him and Jugnu, who were ages apart, with an entire generation between them. *Strange*, Ojhai thought sometimes, *how seclusion brought people together*.

So many like Ojhai and Jugnu must have stayed apart yet begun to get close.

'So what's it this time, little fellow?' Ojhai shouted across the fence.

'Corn! Corn!' The little boy waved and shouted, pulling away from his mother and running towards the path. 'Mai had sown some corn. But if there is no rain soon, they won't sprout.' He paused and wiped his nose on his arm before explaining, 'The hens keep clawing there; they will eat up the corn.' He perched himself on the charpoy once again, helping

Batloo up with him, and said, 'Mai was digging, looking for some yam roots.'

'Found any?' Ojhai asked.

The boy shook his head. 'Fresh, tender curls of dhenkia ferns too won't show up without the rains. How I love to eat them!' he said, smacking his lips, shutting his eyes and wringing his hands. 'Do you too?' he asked Ojhai.

'Huh? Oh, yeah, yeah,' Ojhai nodded, 'I do too!'

'But, you know,' the child continued, 'even the wild taro and arum are fast getting exhausted. Mai said if the rains don't come in a few days, I'll get to eat only rice and salt.'

Tara could no longer go out in search of daily wage work because of the nationwide lockdown that was in place to check people from getting infected with the satanic virus that was fast spreading its tentacles. So, even if a few shops did have a measly stock of pulses and oils, Tara had no money to buy them. Now she had to depend solely on the relief packages from the government, the herbs and roots from the wild, the eggs from her hens, and a little milk from the goat for Jugnu.

'Had your meal today, son?' Ojhai asked, feeling sad and curious.

Jugnu nodded. Even before Ojhai could sigh in relief, the little boy added, 'But Mai didn't.'

'Why so?' Ojhai asked.

'There was enough only for one. Either Batloo or her.'

Against the wall, in the shade of the hut, Ojhai saw the dog eating from a leaf.

Jugnu went on, 'And Mai can go to fetch grains only tomorrow.' He thought for a moment and then said, 'No, not tomorrow. The day after. Yes.'

Ojhai couldn't exactly place since when he had started seeing Tara around in that yard. He had never noticed, not till then. He didn't even know that Marcus's son Birju had brought in a bride, for there had been no music, no festivity, no hustle of people and relatives. People said that she just came in with Birju and stayed on.

Ojhai's daughter-in-law had just then put some rice and a few potatoes in a bag and put it across the fence.

'Nei, Jugnu!' she called out cheerfully. 'Here, run up and carry this to your Mai.'

The boy immediately hopped and skipped up to the fence, followed by an entourage of dog, goat and hens, picked up the bag and ran back into the house, calling for his mother. Ojhai kept watching. When the boy came out, he brought something in his hands and raised it for Ojhai to see. He climbed onto the charpoy and held the object above his head. It took Ojhai a while to recognize what it was.

'Why! Now isn't that a serja?' Ojhai exclaimed.

'Yes, that!' the child replied, equally thrilled.

Ojhai's heart began to beat fast. 'And whose?' But he already knew.

'Mai said my grandfather used to play this,' Jugnu said, examining the serja, 'though she never saw him.'

Ojhai could almost hear the notes of the serja from the child's hands resonating through the corridors of his memory, long buried but unearthed once more that instant. How many Bwisagus had they—he, Marcus, Daimalu and Birkhang—danced the bagurumba together! So many nights had they got merrily drunk on jou under the starlit sky of Madlagami. And then the riots happened. Like the pandemic that year, the riots too had snuffed out the gaiety and festivity of Bwisagu many years ago, driving a wedge between two beautiful people. Those too were Bwisagus when people stayed indoors for fear of their lives. Those too were Bwisagus when, instead of the notes of the siphoong and serja and beats of the kham, what persistently rang through the air were blasts of crude homemade hand grenades and gunshots. Madlagami and the neighbouring villages no more remained what they used to be. Ojhai's reverie broke with Jugnu's call.

'Can you play this too?' the little boy was shouting. 'But the strings are all broken.'

'Well, no, child. I can't play that,' Ojhai's thoughts paused as he turned his attention to the child, who was looking longingly at the instrument in his hand. Not wishing to dampen the little boy's spirits, Ojhai added, 'But if I get the strings mended, once the disease ceases and the lockdown is over, would you like to try your hand at it, Jugnu?'

'Ahaa! Can I?' he asked eagerly. 'Mai once said she kept it carefully so that I could play it someday ... You know what?'

'What?'

'She said it held memories. She said it was the only thing left in the house for me to connect with my father and grandfather,' he paused and asked Ojhai: 'You understand connect?'

'Now what is connect?' Ojhai wondered what innocent interpretation the child might have of it.

'Connect,' he repeated, taking his right palm above his heart with the other hand and gently placing it there, 'like this!'

'But of course!' Ojhai nodded slowly. 'I do get it now. Connect, yes!' While the little boy touched his heart in his yard, it filled Ojhai's to the brim, back in his own yard across the path, despite the separation. Connect. That's what it was.

'Birju, your father, did he play for you?' Ojhai asked when he found his voice.

'Birju?' the little boy asked.

Ojhai understood it wasn't often that he heard his father's name. Maybe never.

'I don't remember him,' Jugnu replied. 'Mai says I was still suckling at her breast when the spirits took him away.' He paused and looked down at the serja. 'Can you mend this?'

'Not really,' Ojhai replied, 'but I guess I can get my friend to help us out. And then if he agrees, you may learn to play it from him.'

'Then maybe you and I can play together, eh, Abou?' he asked enthusiastically. 'You, the siphoong and I, the serja?'

That day, for the first time ever, Jugnu had addressed Ojhai thus. Abou. Grandfather.

'And why not!' Ojhai found his voice choking. 'That will be one of the best Bwisagus ever. What say, little Jugnu?'

'Jugnu says yes!' Saying this, he jumped down from the charpoy and, holding the serja high with Batloo leaping after him, began to skip in circles around the yard singing a Bwisagu song, in Bodo.

*I'll turn a youth when Bwisagu comes,*
*I'll dig for you Ayei juicy arum,*
*Weave me a phali, the old's all a-shred,*
*Draping it, I'll fetch, kopou for your head.*
*While you dance, I'll play the serja,*
*Bagurum bagurum bagurumba!*

Beside himself with joy, Jugnu shouted out to Ojhai, 'Oihoi, Abou! Bring in your siphoong!'

'Why, sure!' Ojhai shouted back.

And their two yards came alive with the notes of Bwisagu ringing into the air. When Ojhai let his siphoong whistle out a Bwisagu melody, the new, fluroscent-green leaves on the boughs of trees tickled the romancing birds hiding among them to make them sing in glee too. The buds of orchids began to open and bloom. The evening sky of spring turned dark enough to shield lovers in embrace, but starlit enough for them to gaze into each other's eyes and feel their hearts beat against one another's. For the rest, it brought upon the senses a blissful delirium that made the feet tap and the heart dance. Such was the magic of the Bwisagu music that Ojhai and his siphoong created.

Just then, he noticed Jugnu running up to the fence with a pouch made from a large leaf that was tied with a reed. He carefully pushed the pouch through the fence into Ojhai's yard, left it on the ground and ran back.

'Take that, Abou!' Jugnu shouted once he got back to his own yard. 'Mai sent it.'

'And what's in there?' Ojhai asked, taking the siphoong down.

Ojhai's daughter-in-law got up from her loom and walked to the fence to pick it. When she unwrapped the leaf, she found a whole mix of wild herbs and ferns that she would not have been able to gather that year, staying confined to their own fenced yard. And from his yard, once again lifting the serja and hopping about with it, pretending to play it, Jugnu yelled, 'Gwkha gwkhai, Mai said!'

Only when Ojhai heard Jugnu did it dawn on him that the next day was the eve of the Bwisagu festivities, the gwkha gwkhai janai day. It was the day they traditionally had a hundred and one herbs and vegetables all cooked together, sometimes even with a few chunks of meat thrown in. The Bodos considered all of those herbs to have medicinal value that would bring them good health in the new year. In her own little way, it was as if Tara was spindling in her share of the yarn too, to mend the fabric that promised to hold the Bodos and the Santhals together once more.

Still playing his siphoong, Ojhai danced his way to the open courtyard. From there, he could see and hear Jugnu dancing around, holding the broken serja aloft. Seeing Ojhai's zest, his son came out of the house and walked into the barn. There, he brought the kham down from the rafters, dusted it and checked its flat, leather sides. Then he tested the strength of the belt and, looping it over his head, stepped into the courtyard to join his father.

Ojhai's eyes twinkled. He looked up at the sky. The last rays of the strong sun were slowly slipping away, leaving an orange glow over Madlagami. The notes from his siphoong now changed to cajole and plead with the skies to quench the thirst of the parched earth. So doleful were the notes that they prompted a cuckoo to cry. The more Ojhai pleaded with the skies through his siphoong, the more passionately the cuckoo sang, as if lending its solidarity to Ojhai's plea and strengthening it. Ojhai looked towards the call, but didn't see the bird. Hidden among boughs and leaves, it sang again and again. The siphoong and the bird continued to sing in harmony, pleading with the skies to show mercy and let the rain fall; pleading for Tara and Jugnu, and for so many like them for whom each full meal was a festival in itself—an event to be celebrated even more than Bwisagu itself.

It was after many years that Ojhai's son played the kham that evening. And such a marvellously resounding beat it was! He soon fell in rhythm with his father's siphoong. The combined passion, along with the notes of the cuckoo, set such a racing pulse through the whole of Madlagami and the skies above it that even the heavens began to tremble. Slowly, Ojhai began hearing random Bwisagu beats of the kham rolling in from all around his little village. The blue-throated barbet too pitched in. All of a sudden, he thought he heard the roar of something other than khams. Was it the heavens trembling? He paused playing his siphoong and listened. The sound came from very far but seemed to be approaching. He closed his eyes to listen more intently. The rumbling grew louder as it appeared to come closer. Soon, there was a deafening clap above them. Ojhai jumped with joy.

'Thunder!' he cried with excitement. 'Hear, hear! Thunder!'

His son's hands began falling with greater ecstasy on the kham and, even without Ojhai realizing, he began playing a tune of deep gratitude in anticipation of his pleas being heard. So moving were the strains from his siphoong that they tore through the stubbornness of the skies and made them weep. Finally, heaven's tears fell on the parched earth to quench her thirst. That same instant, Bwisagu arrived at Madlagami!

'Rain! Rain!' Jugnu shouted and jumped with delight.

Ojhai's daughter-in-law couldn't hold herself back. She leapt out of the kitchen and ran into the open courtyard, raising her arms and looking up towards the gathering grey clouds. Large drops of rain fell on her eyes and trickled down her cheeks. They fell on her nose too, and dripped down her lips. She parted them to taste the first showers of spring. Around them, the strains of bagurumba rose from various courtyards all over Madlagami and came together to unite as one voice singing the same ode—of Bwisagu. Every family remained in its own courtyard, but there was no stopping their spirits from coming together and celebrating the New Year with their neighbours. Even as they remained where they were, they all sang and danced, together in spirit, pace and rhythm.

The fragrance of the first rains of the season seeping into the dry earth filled the night air on that eve of Bwisagu. That evening, it smelt better than the most sensuous jasmines.

Wild with joy, Jugnu's sharp voice rose above the noise of the rain and kham, singing songs of Bwisagu along with the Bodos around him.

Bagurumba hai bagurumba
Bagurumba hai bagurumba!
Jath nungabwla kul nungabwla
Thabwrwm homnanwi bamnanwi lagoumwnkha
Hai Bagurumba
Thuri barini lai daosen
Jwngni lagwa lai dajen
Gwsw hwsar hwsar mwsa de
Baidemlai sidemlai mwsa de hai mwsa de
Dwi jiri jiri samo khingkhiri sona ni jinjiri
Bagurumba hai bagurumba
Bagurum bagurum bagurum ba!

*Bagurumba, hai bagurumba,*
*Had we not been*
*Same clan, same family,*
*I'd hold on to you passionately.*
*Hai bagurumba.*
*Like birds in the fallow field,*
*Give up not, folks of our village,*
*Dance with euphoria, dance with grace,*
*Bagurumba, hai bagurumba.*
*Rippling waters of the prancing river,*
*Where snails a-shimmer,*
*Like golden chain a-glitter,*
*Bagurumba, hai bagurumba,*
*Bagurum bagurum bagurumba!*

For the first time since Ojhai had begun noticing Jugnu, Tara and their small but happy yard brimming with fowl and mammals, he saw Tara happy. She was crying tears of joy as she danced, going round and round with her little son, holding his hands, and then lifting him high above her head to make him feel the rain she had been so eagerly waiting for. The corn she had planted would now start growing. The dhenkia ferns would now sprout new, tender curls and there would be new stalks of arum and taro. She cried and laughed at the same time, swirling Jugnu in the rain as the little boy sang and shrieked with joy. Ojhai thought he saw a flicker appear at the threshold to Tara's house and in that flicker, he felt he saw Marcus sitting on the threshold, playing his serja. His own siphoong too continued to whistle untiringly, pausing only when Ojhai paused for breath. While his daughter-in-law danced in his courtyard, Tara danced in hers. They were two people in two yards separated by a path, but the song they each danced to was the same. Of Bwisagu and rejuvenation. The little boy they both loved was the same too.

'Because love is the same, Ojhai,' Marcus had once said, after the two had had a merry swig together, during a Bwisagu many years ago, 'whether it is a Bodo heart,' and he prodded Ojhai in the heart with his finger, 'or a Santhal,' and he brought the finger back to prod his own heart. After all these years, Ojhai once again missed the company of jolly old Marcus on Bwisagu. And now, as they rejoiced and danced, even the rain that soaked them was the same.

Ojhai wished Daimalu and Birkhang were with him. But he knew, among the happy voices that floated through the rain were his friends' too. Through its forced isolation, the pandemic had brought them all together. It gave them all the chance to appreciate the value of everything they took for granted.

Ojhai's daughter-in-law danced in happy abandon. She had finished weaving her phalis. The next day, she would gift one each to her younger brother-in-law, her husband and to Ojhai. And a special, small one to Jugnu. Back in her yard, Tara swirled and danced in the rain till her hair fell loose from the bun it was rolled into and clung to the wet shirt on her back. Just like the rain-soaked earth, youth and womanhood burst through her drenched clothes. Ojhai never saw a happier bagurumba being danced; he never felt Bwisagu touch his soul with greater spirit, essence and belonging.

And his siphoong continued to spin out its magic, imploring the skies not to stop raining on them, so that the folks of Madlagami got a reason to celebrate and carry on their bagurumba even in that spring of seclusion.

# Chapter 6

# WHISKY IN THE RAIN

The brilliant sun over the weekly market at Pandupur was suddenly marred by the thick, grey clouds that barged into the sky from the south. Ojhai looked up.

*Oh no! Looks like it's going to rain*, he panicked. He had not brought his umbrella. Nor had Birkhang or Daimalu. For when they set out for the market in the morning, the sky was a clear blue and held the promise of a sunny day. There was not a speck of even a white cloud. And then this.

Daimalu was haggling over a kilo of deep purple, luscious brinjals.

'Quick, friend, before the rain starts!' Ojhai hurried him.

No sooner had he said that than a large drop of rain fell on his nose. Birkhang's bag was already heavy with a pumpkin, a one-litre coke bottle of mustard oil and a bamboo hollow of fermented fish. Ojhai had bought two kilos of the red, sticky rice and some jaggery, for his daughter-in-law wished to make rice cakes. He was also looking for a good dao, but now the market was turning into a hub of commotion. Vendors sitting in rows under the open sky were hurriedly bundling their wares and shoving themselves into the few thatch sheds that already had their designated vendors sitting inside with their wares. A few umbrellas swung open above people's heads. Some began scurrying towards the large bakul tree at the back of the market to stand under its leafy, wide boughs, hoping for some shelter. Soon, the whole place got noisier with sacks being dragged, feet moving faster and people in general shouting instructions and being helpful—not that it helped much! Some began to hurry towards the few battery-powered rickshaws that were parked on the highway to ferry villagers.

'Eh, Ojhai, leave your dao for the next market day,' Birkhang suggested. 'Let's hurry and get into one of the rickshaws now. Fast!'

The raindrops were getting smaller but had begun falling more rapidly. There was thunder too, at a distance. All this while, Ojhai's siphoong was tucked into the aronai around his waist. But fearing its getting wet, he removed it from there and deftly slid it under his shirt, into the tuck of the phali at his waist. The three men then staggered as fast as their old feet would take them, carrying their bags along. The rain didn't look like it fell accidently and would thus, as abruptly and apologetically, wind up the drops and leave. Instead, it looked menacingly happy, and adamant on pouring long enough for everyone and everything to get drenched. The sky only grew darker with the arrival of more thick clouds.

Up on the highway, people were fast piling into the few waiting rickshaws and, one by one, these began whirring away down the road through the rain.

'Oi! Oi!' Birkhang shouted at the puller of the last, lone rickshaw. 'Keep that one for us, will you? We're three. With our bags.' He shifted his bag to the other hand and waved, 'Oi! Wait, we're coming. Almost there.' However, it took them a while to climb the short uphill track from the market ground to the highway. More so because the rain had made the track slippery. But when they finally reached the rickshaw, they saw that two young girls, a couple of quarrelling children and an elderly woman had already climbed in and were seated, along with another elderly, robust woman who was just halfway in. She had one foot up in the rickshaw and the other down on the ground, showing the skin of her bare leg underneath her dokhona as far high as the men dared to see, much to their embarrassment. She was poised thus because her umbrella was stuck and wouldn't close. As she struggled with it, she rained some choice abuse on someone called Mebla for sending that umbrella with her.

Ojhai turned to Daimalu and whispered, 'Doesn't look like we'll find space here.'

'It doesn't,' Daimalu repeated, shaking his head.

'What, eh?' Birkhang yelled at the rickshaw puller. 'We hailed you from theerrre…' he stretched the last word, turning back and pointing towards the market, 'and then you see young ladies and give them preference, hah?' The corners of the poor rickshaw puller's mouth drooped. 'But … Abou…' he said as the rain began falling harder around him, 'They came and sat before I could say anything.'

The stout lady was still shaking and thumping her umbrella, but now both her feet were in the rickshaw and her rear was comfortably placed on the seat. She, however, continued with the abuse and held her half-open umbrella out of the rickshaw.

'Hop in, hop in,' she said, in between her cursing. So, none of the men realized that she had asked them to hop in. And they remained standing out in the rain while Birkhang continued to argue with the rickshaw puller. A distant thunder roared, prompting the woman to roar even louder: 'Hop in, I say, you oldies! Deaf or what, you! If I leave your old bones drenching, and if those ageing lungs catch the pneumonia, pray all blame will come to me. Hop in!' She almost appeared to have done a favour to Ojhai, Birkhang and Daimalu. 'There now, kids,' she barked at the children, 'climb on to whatever lap you can.' The kids complied.

Some shuffling and nudging vacated a little space, but enough only for two. Daimalu and Ojhai climbed in. The rickshaw puller turned around and looked at the passengers. When he saw that there was no more room at the back but one more passenger was waiting to be seated, he moved aside on his seat and smiling apologetically at Birkhang, said, 'Come, sit, Abou.' But Birkhang was already on the seat next to him even before the words were uttered. For support, he put an arm around the rickshaw puller. In an instant, they were friends. Behind them, the lady gave up trying to shut her errant umbrella, letting it pop out of the rickshaw like the head of a gleeful child from the window of a bus. All of their feet were lifted and placed at weird positions and angles since they also had to accommodate their shopping bags in the foot-space. Nevertheless, the rickshaw rolled out on the highway. The rain pelted outside. And inside, Ojhai's knees were jammed against those of the lady with the umbrella. He felt his siphoong poking his belly and that, somehow, made him feel better.

'So, where to?' asked the rickshaw puller.

'Haldibari,' said the woman with the umbrella.

'Madlagami,' said Birkhang.

Both spoke at the same instant.

'Oh! But they go separate ways!' The rickshaw puller sounded nervous, anticipating another round of squabbling. 'It's a straight road till Sijubagan. But from there, the road to Madlagami turns right and that to Haldibari goes left. So, well, you kind of have time till we reach Sijubagan to decide who takes the rickshaw from there on,' he suggested.

The passengers fell quiet, wondering who should get off in the pouring rain at Sijubagan. The children continued pinching and punching furtively while the rickshaw whizzed through the rain.

Just as the rickshaw neared Sijubagan, the rain rose to a crescendo. Then, spent and exhausted, it began to cease. By the time the rickshaw reached the Sijubagan police outpost, it was a mere drizzle.

Ojhai thrust his hand out and felt the rain. 'Eh, good,' he said. 'This much we can manage, can't we? Let's get off.' He looked at Daimalu and tapped Birkhang on the shoulder.

'Why, sure we can,' Birkhang replied. 'So then, sister,' he addressed the woman with the umbrella, 'you get going in the rickshaw. That'll keep the children dry too.'

The rickshaw pulled to the side at the crossroads, some distance from the police outpost at Sijubagan. Ojhai released his knees from the awkward position in two massive jerks that catapulted him right onto the road, bag and all. Daimalu and Birkhang were already out.

'Might you need the umbrella?' the woman offered.

'Habab! Thanks,' Daimalu said looking up at the sky. 'Doesn't look like there'll be more rain; not till we reach home.'

'Good, then. Get going!' she shouted back as the rickshaw drove away.

'Phew! Some woman, that!' Daimalu sighed and the others roared with laughter.

'But hey! Wait a moment,' Ojhai stopped in his tracks. '"Some woman, that," did you say?'

Daimalu too paused and nodded.

'Precisely!' Ojhai said, thrilled. 'I'd been wondering all along if I had seen her someplace. Sometime. Even that last time you had exclaimed exactly in these words: *some woman, that*! Yeah, that's what you said, remember, Daimalu?' He paused and then suddenly with greater thrill, almost shouted, 'Whisky woman! That's who she was! Yes indeed! Remember? She whisked away the whisky from right under the whiskers of the policeman!'

'Atta boy! Nwngou! Yeah, yeah!' Birkhang's eyes glinted with recollection. 'My! That must've been some ten years back, eh?'

'Some whisky she bestowed upon us!' Ojhai laughed, remembering the moment. 'Now that we met her today, who knows, we may once more chance upon good old Bhutanese whisky, just like that day!' The men guffawed as they trudged on with their bags.

It was still drizzling when the three friends walked past the police outpost. Its large compound was empty that day, except for a few goats nibbling at the juicy blades of tender grass that the monsoon had given birth to. There was an old Mahindra Bolero—used by the officer-in-charge of the outpost as his allotted official vehicle—parked near the wall. The men could also see the once-white Maruti Suzuki Omni that had been lying in the outer yard for around a decade now. Many years ago, it had been pulled in by a crane and dumped there. Its metal body was rusted in large patches all over, and the sliding doors were gone. One of the past officers in charge had them stolen and sold, and extracted a share of the loot

… or so people gossiped. One of the tyres met the same fate, they whispered. The other three were now flatter than a rolling board. The van had sunk into the ground from years of standing and doing nothing; going nowhere. And a merry bunch of wild creepers took it upon themselves to entangle and hold the van from sinking further. Some even said that spirits had made it their dwelling.

Meanwhile, the drizzle was once more gaining momentum. Soon, the skies darkened again. The drizzle was turning into a shower. Ojhai, Daimalu and Birkhang had already walked past the police outpost. Otherwise they could have taken shelter in its wide verandah. And even before they could hasten their steps, the rain quickened its pace. Instinctively, the men began partly running and partly walking. 'But where to?' Ojhai asked. 'There!' Daimalu replied, pointing towards the skeletal Omni. So all three plodded towards the van as fast as they could.

'Phew! Never thought this scrap would come to our rescue,' Birkhang said, climbing onto the backseat and wiping his head and face with his aronai. Daimalu climbed in next to him, wringing the lower edge of his phali. And Ojhai found himself in the driver's seat. They all put their bags down by their feet and made themselves as comfortable as was possible in a tin box that was falling apart and probably housed spirits.

'What now?' Daimalu asked.

'Sit and wait,' Ojhai replied, 'for the rain to stop.'

So they sat and waited. In silence. Listening to the rain drumming on the tin roof of the van.

Suddenly, Birkhang exclaimed, 'Eh, remember the day we first saw this car? Abandoned on the highway, with the boot stacked with crates and crates of Zumzin and K5? Bah! Bhutan sure knows how to brew her peach wine and her whisky!'

Daimalu slapped his thigh in zestful recollection. 'Some commotion that was! Yeah, I remember. And the driver had fled, leaving the van unattended because the police had waylaid him.'

'What was the waylaying for? I didn't quite get it that day either, never got it till now. What was it for?' Birkhang asked.

'Why!' Ojhai quipped. 'Didn't you hear the constable on guard say that day? For not having the papers required to carry such a large amount of the good stuff? And also because it was all foreign stuff.'

Birkhang nodded. 'Whoa! How smart she was, then … this old tin box,' he said, now tapping at the sides of the car. 'And some crowd it was, that had gathered around it. But, boy! It was today's umbrella woman who stole the show even that day. Remember how she brought things round to be at her command?' The men nodded vigorously, sighed and agreed.

Daimalu added excitedly: 'Oi, listen! Remember Rolen trying to smuggle out a crate when he got to know it was whisky? And then got whacked in the butt by the policeman?' The men roared with laughter. And suddenly, the old tin box came alive. Like some ten years ago on the highway.

'There!' The lone constable had shouted that day on the highway with immense authority, wielding his lone weapon—the lathi. He was so lanky that they feared he might fall forward at any moment owing to the disproportionate thickness of his moustache. 'Now don't go close to the car! Get off there!' The little children who were running their greasy, sweaty palms along the sleek body of the vehicle collectively glided back. Ojhai, Birkhang and Daimalu were standing a few feet away, but were very much a part of the cluster of curious onlookers. Those days, their ears and eyes were ten years younger. So even from where they stood, they took in every turn of event with immense clarity and delight.

'What are those at the back?' someone asked.

'Ah, those?' The constable twirled his moustache. 'Those are crates of Bhutan's famous peach wine. It's written large and clear.' Pointing towards the name on one of the boxes with his lathi, he read out: 'Zumzin. Can't you read?'

The crowd collectively repeated, 'Zumzin,' dwelling lengthily on the 'm' and 'n', and nodding at one another.

'But,' asked a little boy, 'there's a 5 with the K. Over there, in that box.'

'Oh, that? You ignoramuses!' The constable shifted his lathi from the crate of Zumzin to a different one now, a green one. 'That's a different drink, with a different name. Now read this...' he once again pointed with his lathi. 'K5. That's the first-ever whisky that Bhutan brewed. It's named after their fifth king.'

Collective 'ohs' and 'ahs' arose from the crowd in awe of the policeman's fine knowledge of the drinks of a foreign nation. He, on the other hand, felt grateful for having managed to eavesdrop on the conversation of the sub-divisional police officer of Gossaigaon who had driven all the way to take stock of things and report to the superintendent of police at Kokrajhar. After the initial reporting, the officers had got busy arranging for a tow truck to drag the shiny Maruti Suzuki Omni to the outer yard of the Sijubagan police outpost, leaving the constable to ward pesky elements away from the car, and the crates.

On the highway, passing vehicles slowed down to see what the crowd and chaos were about. The constable swung his lathi and motioned them to move on and not create traffic hold ups. Little boys gaped at him and his power in amazement, wondering if they could ever become like him when they grew up.

'Honeii! Police!' a lady had called out above the din and commotion. The constable didn't hear. Or conveniently ignored what he heard.

'Honeii!' she called louder. Some giggled.

'Hm? Can't you see I'm on duty?' the constable responded smugly, turning around to see who had the audacity to call him thus. But when he saw the matronly woman with her generous girth and no-nonsense face, his smug authority slid down a wee bit.

'Now what?' he asked.

'Now this,' she started. 'So you say there is wine in them,' she said, pointing at a crate of Zumzin through the closed window, 'and whisky there?' She slid her finger across the glass to point at one of the green boxes of K5.

'So I did! Didn't you hear? Expensive liquor, mind you, Madwi, from Bhutan.'

The woman cupped one half of her face with her thumb and fingers along the cheek and stuck her nose onto the glass window like the children around her, to see the insides better.

'Hands off! Noses off!' the constable barked.

'Liquor, eh?' the woman asked again.

'Any doubt?' the constable questioned in reply. 'Can't you see the original boxes with their original labels and names?'

'Eh, I see that, but,' she raised the bottle she was carrying by a loop of rope round its neck, to the level of his eye. 'See this?' she asked.

The constable smirked. 'Pah! You compare a bottle of Liv52 with K5, Madwi? Just because it too has a 5 in it? Heh heh!' And with his free hand he brushed away a non-existent fly above his nose.

'Heh heh!' the woman mimicked. 'It too has a 5, no doubt, but if you're as sure of that original box of K5 containing only K5 whisky, like my original bottle of Liv52 with its original label containing only original liver tonic, then take a good look.' She then held the bottle closer to his eyes and chuckled, 'Kerosene oil! See? In an original bottle of Liv52!' Others around the van giggled into their palms as the constable looked left and right to see if anyone but him had heard her.

'Some woman, that!' Daimalu whispered to Birkhang and Ojhai.

'So?' The constable asked defiantly.

'So this…' she said. 'You ought to check what's actually in those boxes. If it isn't the famous peach wine and whisky from a foreign country, the police higher up the ladder will hold you responsible for the vanished liquor. You see, you may lose your job, my boy.'

Daimalu nudged Birkhang and the two winked.

'Some nerve, eh?' Ojhai whispered to his friends.

That caught the constable off guard. He was in a fix now. Drawing the woman aside, he asked in low tones: 'So, Madwi, what do you think should be done?'

'Simple!' she replied in an equally low tone. 'Take out a crate of each and look inside.'

He nodded, walked to the driver's door, opened it, climbed in and hauled one lanky leg over the front seat to reach the seat at the centre. Leaning his stomach against the backrest, he dangled towards the back to try and tear open the seal of a golden and peach coloured box with 'Zumzin' written on it. The seal did give way, but the crates were so tightly stacked against one another that it was impossible for the constable to pull out a bottle and examine its contents. More so because of the precarious lodging of his lanky body. Moreover, he felt like being stripped naked by the stare of hundreds of eyes from outside the van. Sweating under his khaki shirt, the hapless constable turned and looked out. The first face he saw was of the matronly woman. It surprised him that a wave of relief poured through him on seeing her. She was gesturing through the glass for him to come out.

'Open the back door. Let me help!' she shouted.

The constable slithered back on his belly onto the driver's seat, turned and stepped out of the car. The cool breeze soothed his frayed nerves to some extent. He obeyed the woman. The crowd that clung to the vehicle like fruit flies on overripe banana parted to make way when the constable walked towards the back door of the van. The elderly woman followed him with an air of elevated status. As if in choreographed synchronization, the crowd stepped back to let the two pass, then stepped farther back to let the door swing open. As soon as the constable and the woman put their hands on the crate, the crowd once more stepped in with zeal.

'Hoi! Hoi!' the woman turned round and shouted. 'Push back, will you? None of your business, hoi!'

'Any of yours?' Daimalu called back.

'Hoi, phagla! You crazy fellow!' she retorted with a sheepish grin. 'Can't you see I'm just helping him?'

She nudged the constable and said, 'You take down one crate and put it here, down on the road.' She stepped aside to make room for the crate.

The constable looked at her, perplexed. 'Take out a crate? I'll be jailed! I'll lose my job!'

'Bah! Then go on and try to pull out a bottle from that thick-as-pork-fat stack. Go on! So tightly have they placed the boxes, headless people, whoever! Even the skin doesn't cling to the body that desperately. 'Jamba fwr! Idiots.' And she spat on the ground. 'You'll anyway lose your job and go to jail if it isn't original whisky and wine from Bhutan in those bottles.'

The exasperated constable realized the truth in her words. So he cautiously slid out the top-most crate—emblazoned with the brand name—from the side. It was almost touching the roof of the car.

'Here, pass it to me,' she said stretching out her meaty arms. Then she proceeded to bring it down cautiously and placed it near her feet.

'Now, a green one,' she directed.

It amused Ojhai, Birkhang and Daimalu to see how she had placed herself in command of the situation.

'She sure has some motive!' Ojhai remarked, trying to hold back a laugh.

'You bet!' Daimalu agreed.

Just as the crates were kept down on the road and the woman hunched over them to tear the seal and check the contents, with more than half the onlookers standing on their toes behind them and craning their necks, a siren shrieked. It was coming towards them. The constable jumped up in panic, picked up his lathi and swung it in the air, shouting with alarm, 'Go! Go! Go! Clear the way! Move! Go!' Most onlookers fled, though some trotted to the other side of the road to watch from a distance. The constable could see the tow-away vehicle and the Bolero belonging to the Sijubagan Police outpost's officer-in-charge. On the verge of a nervous breakdown, the constable quickly shut the van's back door. There was no time to put the withdrawn crates back in. He looked helplessly at the woman. She in turn looked at Ojhai, Daimalu and Birkhang.

'Nei!' she hissed, motioning the men to come to her. 'What have you been doing, sturdy males all, standing like loafers and just watching all along while I am single-handedly having to manage the situation! Come, lend me a hand.'

'Wha…?' Birkhang voiced the three men's collective surprise.

'Now stop letting your mouths hang loose in surprise and hide them crates in the thickets over there,' she ordered, motioning towards the bushes along the side of the highway. 'Quick now!'

To their amazement, the men too found themselves complying with her. And the crates were soon out of sight, hidden inside the bushes. So when the officer arrived with the monstrous towtruck, everything was in order.

A few men got off the tow truck and approached the van, pulling hooks attached to sturdy cables. They latched the hooks to grooves in the front of the liquor-filled car and were getting all set to drag the car away. While all this was going on in the highway in full view of the onlookers, elsewhere, off the highway, away from prying eyes, three old men, one elderly woman and a few of her friends were tearing seals off crates that had arrived illegally from neighbouring Bhutan. With all good intentions, of course. Just to check if the contents were truly what they were supposed to be—the finest peach wines and the first-ever brewed whisky from the mountain kingdom.

The contents turned out to be indeed genuine.

But now there was no way for them to put the crates back into the van even if they wished to. So the forlorn oldies glanced at one another and came upon an unspoken understanding, sharing the bottles amongst themselves, save for a couple of bottles in each crate. The elderly woman deftly tucked bottles of both whisky and wine into the folds of her dokhona. When she stood up, besides looking rounder around the middle, there was no trace of any hidden booty on her. The men too tucked bottles into the phali at their waist, let hang their shirts over them and then firmly tied their aronais over the waist—over the loot. And as the van with the crates of Zumzin and K5 was getting towed away, respectably escorted by sirens and the vehicle of the officer-in-charge with the lanky constable in it, the senior folks stepped out of the bushes, paused a while to be part of the van's send-off and then walked away to their respective homes, discussing zealously the adventures of the morning.

There after, joyful evenings passed, for as many evenings as the fine stuff lasted. Every evening, the old men gathered in one of their courtyards and raised a toast. Ojhai played the siphoong while Daimalu and Birkhang broke into impromptu bagurumba. Ah! Such delightful evenings! And on each one of those evenings they blessed the king and kingdom of Bhutan from the bottom of their spirited hearts, for brewing such divine spirit.

'Ah! Such blissful evenings those truly were!' Ojhai reminisced. 'How time flies!'

Rain drummed on the roof of that same van, now reduced to a pathetic ghost of its old, swanky self. No one heard of what happened to the rest of the crates. But many heard of the happy hours that rang out from the residential quarters of the officer-in-charge of the outpost. The lanky constable was spotted by some till a few years ago. Only, he was no more lanky. He was more prosperous around the middle, pompous in his manners, and moved around with the officer-in-charge in his official Bolero.

'Hey!' Birkhang suddenly jumped in his seat. 'Do you think any of them crates might still be sitting around at the back?'

'Want to check?' Daimalu asked.

'Not a bad idea to while away time,' Ojhai added. 'As it is, we can't move out till the rain stops.'

Now it was Birkhang's turn to lean into the back of the van on his stomach, just like the lanky constable did all those years ago. The other two laughed remembering the scene. The back was littered with goat shit. Creepers crawled in through the broken windows and gaps in the frame of the car, and sprawled out on the floor.

'Nothing much that I see,' Birkhang reported. 'But there's some glittering thing blinking in the corner.' He leaned farther towards the back. 'Oi, Ojhai, pass me your siphoong. Let me tap and see what it is.' When he tapped about with the siphoong, it hit something. Something hard. 'Sounds like glass,' he said. He removed the creepers around it and tapped again.

'Hoiyaa! Look! Look! It is! It's one of them! Green!'

The other two turned around excitedly.

'Eh, I forget the name!' Ojhai exclaimed.

'K5!' Birkhang yelled.

But the bottle was wedged in real hard. Both Daimalu and Birkhang had to use all limbs and the siphoong to unwedge it. And when it did, their elation knew no bounds. Because, lodged under the first one, there was a second green bottle, which came off easier than the first.

'Someone must have hidden these here to collect later, at an opportune time,' Daimalu remarked.

'Perhaps. But it's ours now!' Ojhai rejoiced. 'Let's dance the bagurumba, friends! Bagurum bagurum mwsaa deh, hei lwgwphwr!' And Ojhai took the siphoong to his lips.

'Now I see what people meant when they said this tin box was the abode of spirits. Green spirits!' Daimalu exclaimed with joy, raising a bottle of the K5.

Ten years ago, they had learnt that whisky had to be had with water and not raw, like the home-brewed rice beer and Zumzin. Way back then, they sipped it at home where they had glasses to mix the whisky and the water. Now, though, as they wondered what to do, Daimalu yanked off a chunk of leather from the already torn seat and rolled it into a funnel like the ones wayside vendors used to pack and sell roasted grams and peanuts. He folded up the pointed end and held it out in the rain for a cursory rinsing of his leather mug. Then he collected some water there.

'There now,' he said jubilantly, 'pour in the elixir!'

Amid great rejoicing, singing and dancing—the latter only with their upper bodies—the men took turns to sip the famous whisky from the land of the thunder dragon. And while thunder boomed above them, spewing lightning like a dragon would spit fire, the three friends drowned themselves in timelessness and happy oblivion. They never imagined that their tin-box shelter in a torrential downpour would rain such euphoria on them.

'King of Bhutan!' Ojhai shouted with great joy. 'Here we come to thank you! Vroom! Vroom! Brooabrrummmm!' Making the dead engine come to life with his tongue rolling on the roof of his mouth, he turned the steering wheel and, clasping the gear lever, gave it a massive, spirited shove. However, rusted at the base, the long lever broke and came off in his hand. The other two bent over laughing and raised more toasts.

About an hour later, the skies had exhausted their rain and only the last few drops were drizzling. Just so, the jolly men too had exhausted two bottles of K5 whisky, leaving only a pint at the bottom of the second bottle. Even that remained because by then the men were way too drunk to realize that some more was left. Daylight was on the wane and so were their nerves. As happens when drunkenness jumps from one high to the next higher, the men's eyelids were drooping, euphoria was giving way to sadness and Ojhai's siphoong was now whistling out poignant strains that moved the other two to tears.

'Sshh!' Ojhai heard them say.

'Don't sshh me, dear friends,' Ojhai sobbed. 'Let me play my blues!' And he played tunes that pulled at Daimalu's and Birkhang's heartstrings.

'Sshh!'

This time, Ojhai broke down. 'Don't, my dearest friends, don't silence me. Let me unburden my soul!'

As more melancholy floated out of his siphoong, Birkhang turned to Daimalu and, slurring, asked, 'Why did you sshh him? Don't!'

'Eh, I did?' Daimalu sounded surprised. 'But I thought it was you!'

'Oh? None of us did?' Birkhang raised his eyebrows to keep his eyelids from clasping shut.

They stared at each other. 'Then who did?'

'Sshh!'

Together they turned around towards the sound and when they saw what was *sshh-ing*, they froze. They turned to Ojhai and whispered, 'Ojhai, sshh!'

'I mean,' Birkhang bit his tongue and said in the lowest of tones he could emit: 'Stop, Ojhai, stop! There's a snake here. Right behind us.'

'Eh, dear Birkhang, now isn't the time to pull my leg,' Ojhai said, pensive. 'My siphoong is crying out for more soulful melody, as is my heart. Don't stop me, my dear, don't.' Wiping a tear from the corner of his eye with the back of his hand, he touched the siphoong to his lips. Closing his eyes, he resumed playing, swaying ever so slightly with the sorrow after the soar induced by the spirit.

It was only when Daimalu tapped him from behind that he opened his eyes and was left gaping in horror. A snake! A thick, dark one. Entwined around the steering wheel, it raised its head and some six inches of its body below that, and was swaying right in front of Ojhai's nose to the gentle rhythm of the siphoong's movements. Out of sheer terror, Ojhai's fingers lost their grip over the siphoong. It fell under the seat and rolled away out of reach. Instantly, the snake too slithered away, disappearing under the seat. The three men remained paralyzed, scared even to breathe. Under their seats, on the tin floor, they heard the *thrrokitoktokthotok* of the siphoong, rolling farther into the back of the van.

When the snake vanished from sight, Daimalu found his voice. 'Friends! Now, quick!' And he gestured to them to alight from the van. In their journey out of the tin box, he and Birkhang made the stealthiest of movements possible given their state of shock and drunkenness, dragging their shopping bags after them.

'Hurry, walk away!' Birkhang said, taking faltering steps into the drizzle.

Ojhai got down with his bag but, looking back at the van, whispered, 'My siphoong!' He refused to leave without it.

'We'll come again for that, Ojhai, later. For now, for Bathou's sake, come away!' Daimalu tugged at his arm.

But Ojhai suddenly kept the bag on the ground and hurried to the back of the van, to where they had heard the siphoong rolling away.

'Ojhai!' Birkhang shouted. 'You crazy old fool! Have you gone nuts or what? Come back! The fellow's hollow up there,' he said pointing at Ojhai's head, 'just like his siphoong! Come away, Ojhai!'

But Ojhai was hell-bent on taking his siphoong with him. When he peered into the back of the van, he saw the snake coiled around the siphoong and dragging it calmly into the groove where the sliding door rolled long ago. He realized that the siphoong hadn't rolled away there from under the seat on its own. The snake had brought it there. Even in his state of drunken stupor, he realized that it would be challenging to retrieve the siphoong from the clutches of the snake.

'Oi, Ojhai! Come with us, please!' Daimalu shouted.

Instead, Ojhai walked around to the front of the car, picked one of the green bottles and held it up against the light to see if anything was left.

'Heck!' he said, disappointed, and hurled it away. He picked up the other one and stuck the mouth of the bottle into his eye. 'Ah! Some hope here,' he said and held the bottle by the edge of the van's roof to collect some dripping rainwater. Just a bit. For he wanted the blend to give a hard kick instantly. Then, letting the bottle stand on the floor of the van, he found the piece of seat leather which they had earlier rolled and used as a cup. Once again, Ojhai made a funnel of that same piece of leather, tied it to one end of the broken gear lever with a piece of coir that he pulled out from the seat and cautiously poured the whisky from the bottle into that funnel. His mind was working, though languidly, only thanks to his love for the siphoong. His vision, on the other hand, came and went, and as he stood, his body swayed to and fro too. He took a good, deep breath to muster up his courage and steady his limbs. Then carrying the gear lever, he walked around to the back of the van to where the snake was romancing his siphoong, and held out the whisky to the reptile.

'This dimwit will get all three of us bitten today!' Birkhang mumbled.

Its head high and its tongue flicking, the snake took a swift swing towards the intruder, but its tail possessively held on to the siphoong. Ojhai then made the gear lever with the whisky-filled funnel lean upright against the inside of the car and, having left it standing there, stepped aside and waited. Still and quiet. Meanwhile, some distance away, Birkhang and Daimalu held on to each other for support, flinging all kinds of obscenities as well as words of encouragement at Ojhai. Sometimes they doubled up over a guffaw and sometimes straightened up with sympathy, but never left Ojhai's side. The snake slowly inched towards the whisky. It paused, looked around for possible threat and when it found none, took a quick flick from the leather funnel. The pungent taste made it jerk its head back. It swayed a bit before slowly moving towards the whisky again. This time, it licked up all of it and stared out into the drizzle, its head still high, its tail still curled around the siphoong. Ojhai held his breath and watched. Till now, his plan was working well. A while later, the snake gently lowered its head and loosened its grip around the siphoong. Ojhai felt like he had been standing there for an eternity. Soon, the snake put its head on the floor of the van and though it had uncoiled its tail from the siphoong, it lay close to it, limp and drunk.

Ojhai cautiously moved forward and, with great stealth, pulled away the siphoong. In its place, he quietly slipped in the gear lever. He shoved the siphoong into his phali and, tip-toeing to his bag, he picked it up and the men fled. Groggy heads, loaded bags and unstable legs on a squishy, rain-soaked mud road with big puddles of rainwater did very little to help them quicken their pace homeward. Every now and then, one of them turned back to see if the snake was following them to stake claim on the siphoong. It did not.

And the men trudged a long and arduous track home—one that was much longer than usual.

On reaching Madlagami, from the turn of the path under the large ficus, the friends parted for their respective homes. Nothing much by way of byes was shouted that day, for everything still seemed to be so distant and dream-like. The effects of Bhutan's royal spirit had not yet gone away completely.

Back at home, Ojhai could barely manage to leave the bag from the market at the doorway to the kitchen and walk to the well for a wash. From there, he staggered straight to his room, got into bed and, having carefully placed the siphoong by his pillow for safekeeping from the snake, dropped off to instant sleep. What a sound sleep that was! His snores were heard right across the courtyard, in the kitchen, as he slept through the night like a baby. In his dreams, the snake had followed him home, dragging the gear lever with it all the way from the rusted, skeletal van in Sijubagan. It also slithered into his room through the narrow gap under the door, neatly pulling the gear lever in with itself. It all seemed so real that even in his dream, he thought he actually heard the lever knock against the wooden door as it was being manoeuvred in. He thought his sleep broke for an instant. His head felt heavy. He didn't know how late into the night it was, but all was still and dark. His hand instinctively felt for the siphoong by his pillow. It was there, safe, lying just as he left it. And he went back to sleep.

Next morning, Ojhai woke up to the sound of loud, frantic knocking on his door.

'Apha! Apha!' It was his son calling from outside. 'Are you alright, Apha?' He sounded anxious. 'You missed supper last night and slept long and late. Apha, are you not well?' There was a pause before he knocked and called again: 'Apha?'

Ojhai sat up in bed. It took him some time to take stock of wakefulness. Slowly, one by one, the abandoned car, the whisky, the snake, all came back to him. He reached for his siphoong and brought it out. It felt cold and smooth. When he looked down at it, whatever little drunkenness was still sitting on him shot out of his head like a pebble from a slingshot. For what he held in his hand was the gear lever.

His siphoong was gone!

Ojhai, Daimalu and Birkhang would, for all their remaining lives, regale folks with this tale of whisky in the rain.

# Chapter 7

# NURTURE

The Baokhungri Hills at Chakrashila always gave Ojhai an eerie feeling of the unseen, unheard presence of someone—a princess, maybe—lurking around him, begging him to play his siphoong.

He had trekked up the hill many a time during his youth, sometimes alone and with Birkhang and Daimalu at other times. Those days, the hills were quiet. Not too many people trudged up—not even on the eve of Bwisagu as they did now. Maybe the hills those days were still mourning Princess Diplai. Back then, when Ojhai sat near Shiv Bwrai's old temple at the peak and played his siphoong, the notes echoed through the stillness of the valley and rolled down to reach Lake Diplai at the foothills, creating ripples in the waters there. The lake too was named after the princess. Ever since then, he had sensed someone around him, someone without a mortal body. Maybe it was just in his mind; maybe it was the tranquillity of the hills that made him feel thus. Whatever be the reason, he felt it all the same.

Today, of course, Ojhai, Birkhang and Daimalu met at the turn of the road under the old ficus and were walking towards the police outpost at Sijubagan. After ages, they would once again trek up the Baokhungri Hills.

It so happened that a motley group of adventure seekers, mostly young, had taken a Tata Winger on hire to take them to the foothills of Baokhungri at Chakrashila and also arranged to take a few musicians with them to kindle their spirits and energize their limbs. Since it was the eve of Bwisagu, some dancing and music were naturally looked forward to. However, an emergency of sorts occurred when just a couple of days before the scheduled day of the trek, the young boy who was hired to play the siphoong went missing. Much searching, investigation and enquiry later, it came to light that the boy had eloped with his lady love, leaving the trekkers without a flautist. It was then that someone came up with Ojhai's name.

'He's a legend when it comes to playing the siphoong,' Rwngwra said, 'and he's a gem of a person too.'

'Ah yes! Abou Siphoong of Madlagami?' Maikhoong added. 'Great suggestion, Rwngwra. But isn't he old? Will he be able to trek up?'

'Bah! He's old but he's a sport,' Gaorao assured the gang.

And that's how they had decided to invite Ojhai to be a part of their hajw gakhwnai festivity on the eve of that Bwisagu—to climb up the forested Baokhungri Hills to worship at the Shiv Bwrai Temple at Hatimatha, as the peak was known. Ojhai readily agreed. His lone condition was that his two inseparable friends Birkhang and Daimalu would come as well.

'Hey! The more the merrier, Abou! They sure are welcome!' Maikhoong had agreed with joy.

And so it was that the three friends were now walking up to the police outpost at Sijubagan, dressed in their Bwisagu best. From there, Maikhoong and his group of trekkers would pick them. Today, Ojhai carried one of his long, festive siphoongs. And in a cotton sling bag, among other knick-knacks, he carried a small, five-holed siphoong too, as a spare one.

'You know, fellas,' Daimalu said as they walked towards the pick-up point, 'climbing the Baokhungri Hills is no more what it used to be back in our time. Remember? Those days, there were just a handful of believers who climbed up the serene hills to pay obeisance to Bathou in His modest temple and pour milk on the stone trunk of the elephant head. Ah! Such peace prevailed! It seeped into the soul. For company, you had only the langurs swinging along the dense boughs overhead. No wonder the princess loved spending time in those idyllic hills.'

'Nwngou lei!' Ojhai nodded. 'These days, it seems almost like a fair all the way up—from the foothills to Hatimatha peak. And what a throng of young trekkers! Boy!'

Daimalu nudged Ojhai and chuckled: 'Those are all young lovers, you see, Ojhai, not grey heads like us. They climb the hills because of the belief that you find true and everlasting love if you walk up the hill to the Shiv Bwrai Temple for three consecutive Bwisagus.'

'Love birds all, eh?' Birkhang laughed. 'Never mind them. There'll be some old mules like us as well. Heh heh! And who knows, we might just come out as second-time lucky in love too!' And the old friends laughed heartily, shoving and elbowing one another in jest.

'And isn't it amazing…' Daimalu recollected, 'Asidoh Buri, the talebearer, I hear, is still there, regaling visitors with her precise chronicles. Habab! Never old, never young. She's another enigma … like the hills themselves.'

As the highway beyond the police outpost came to view, they saw the Winger slowing down and pulling up to the side of the road. Ojhai, Birkhang and Daimalu quickened their steps towards it, for they didn't want to delay the trekking enthusiasts. It was a fine, cool morning, and they would take another half an hour or maybe a little more to reach Chakrashila. They wouldn't mind a little sun because the hills were anyway wooded and there would be plenty of shade and breeze. But then, in such wooded hills, day waned early too, because daylight began to dim rapidly the moment the sun sank behind the hills. So now they hastened towards the Winger, not wishing to cause delay.

'No hurry, Abou! Careful with your steps!' Gaorao shouted, stepping out of the vehicle. 'You're our star musician today. We can't afford to whizz off without you anyway!'

'Ye! Ye! Welcome, Abou Siphoong!' a few young boys shouted from inside the minibus, thrusting their heads out of the windows.

Ojhai, Birkhang and Daimalu could feel the festive spirit in the minibus spilling out of the windows. They felt young once again—like in the days of yore when they walked and cycled all the way to the foothills of Baokhungri and then climbed up the silent hill. Thinking of those days, Ojhai began to wonder if he would still get goose bumps after all these years, whether he would still sense the long-gone princess walk beside him, wishing to hear him play the siphoong. But then he thought the hills wouldn't be tranquil and solitary, not that day. And would a spirit come to be by him in the midst of such noise and commotion? He wasn't even sure if it was a spirit that he felt hovering around him, following him. Wasn't it all just in his mind? It was only the way he felt. A weird intuition, an uncanny sensation, that's all. Or so he forced himself to think. But he shivered nevertheless, when he remembered having felt a soft, breezy touch on his arms once, as if someone—a really light being—had brushed against him as it swayed past.

'Today, it's going to be different,' he told himself.

The three men stepped on board the Winger and the engine roared back to life as the vehicle resumed its drive to Chakrashila.

Once they reached, it amazed Ojhai, Daimalu and Birkhang to see the change that had come over the hajw gakhwnai traditions. Solemn customs had given way to massive festivities over the years. A milling crowd now thronged the otherwise quiet and uninhabited forests, climbing the hills, more for adventure and less because of reverence. It astonished them further to see Nepalese and Bhutanese people in that multitude, standing out in their traditional attire, immersed in tasting the ethnic Bodo delicacies that were being prepared and sold side by side with those that local women folk had brought prepared from their homes, like rice cakes, jou and fermented fish in bamboo hollows. Even that early in the day, some were already returning from Hatimatha, named so because the peak of the Baokhungri Hills looked like an elephant's head from afar. At the foothill was a marquee with details about a cultural programme in the evening.

Young boys and girls had already begun their trek, most of them singing and dancing, some hand in hand and yet others giggling into their palms and allowing themselves just so much of discreet, harmless flirting. Even amongst them, there were those who were climbing the hill with gratitude in their hearts for wishes fulfilled and yet others with devotion, prayers and pleas seeking wishes to be granted. Some came solely to see Asidoh Buri and to hear from her the heart-rending tales surrounding the Baokhungri Hills—tales of Princess Diplai and the love she killed herself for, upon those fateful hills. But it placated Ojhai to see that the hills themselves hadn't changed. They remained—despite all the years and storms that had passed over them—as rugged, old and poised as before, letting large rocks bear down on them and deep roots of aged trees claw into their bosom. The Baokhungri Hills continued to stand stoically protective over the caves and tunnels that cut through it, standing tall as the custodian of many a lore and legend.

Ojhai and the team too got ready to begin their climb. Mergao checked his kham, Leben adjusted his serja and Ojhai readied his siphoong.

'All set?' Maikhoong asked his group. The others nodded, turning to one another, excited and feeling the same renewal of life in their veins that Bwisagu brought to the forests in the hills. Young and old, they all felt a sudden spurt of adrenaline urging them to begin the climb without delay.

'Jai Shiv Bwrai!' Maikhoong hailed.

Ojhai bowed to the hills and began whistling into the siphoong. On a clear day, from Kokrajhar town, the peak of those hills appeared like a mahout riding an elephant. And it was because of the huge white rock which resembled an elephant's forehead that the peak was also called mwiderkhafal. Below mwiderkhafal ran a deep, long tunnel resembling an elephant's trunk. Since the days of yore, people from the neighbouring villages poured milk there on the last day of the month of Chaitra on the eve of Bwisagu, so that it flowed down to Lake Diplai. They believed that if the milk reached the lake named after the princess, the New Year would bring them bounty and good tidings. Birkhang once even swore that fish from that lake had the flavour of milk.

Walking uphill that day after many a Bwisagu and a good part of their lives having passed them by, from youth to grandfatherhood, Ojhai, Daimalu and Birkhang were once again on the lap of the Baokhungri Hills. It felt strange. It felt nostalgic. It felt wonderful. Many a memory of those hills—some happy, some sad—flashed across their minds. The hills had treasured all of them, calmly and ungrudgingly, carefully keeping every secret to themselves.

As Ojhai's notes meandered through the happy cacophony of a horde of trekkers singing songs of Bwisagu to the accompaniment of the serja and japkhring, the breath of the hills seemed to slow down till it came to match the pace of Ojhai's notes. The hills and the siphoong soon began to breathe in the same rhythm as the breeze in the hills began to quicken and slow down with the rise and fall of the siphoong's pitch. Gradually, all other noise seemed to recede into the faraway valleys. The whole of Chakrashila fell silent to listen to Ojhai's siphoong. A troop of langurs was chatting noisily as the monkeys swung above the revellers, mimicking some and scaring others. Even they hushed up, as the hills seemed to slowly plunge into a silence of awe and admiration despite all the festive activity. Just as Ojhai was once again lost in his siphoong, he began to feel the eeriness of an unearthly being hovering about him all over again. And of princess Diplai imploring him to play his siphoong for her. It shook him out of his bliss and he paused. He looked all around him. Everything was just the same. A jolly festive spirit reigned. He wasn't alone; there was no princess.

'Hoi, Abou,' said a man as he passed by, 'go on, keep playing. You almost brought tears to my eyes.'

'Don't stop, Abou. Play on. You inspire our zeal,' said a little girl who was joyously skipping past them.

Ojhai nodded and smiled in acknowledgement, but said he needed to pause for air, to fill his lungs and his siphoong.

'Buddy, you alright?' Daimalu whispered into Ojhai's ear.

'Whaa…h?' Ojhai was embarrassed. 'Oh, yes, yes! I'm fine.'

'You want to rest a while?' Birkhang asked.

'Paah, come on now!' Ojhai shook his head. 'Why the fuss? We just need a refill. Of air. My siphoong and I.' And he feigned breathlessness. For he didn't want anyone to suspect the way he felt about this presence he was now becoming more and more aware of.

And so they trudged on, with Maikhoong leading them. The young among them were immersed in tireless dancing as they walked their way up. Mergao and Leben kept up the zeal of their teammates with deep rumbles of the kham and the sensuous melody of the serja. They walked past women folk who sat by the sides of the foot track selling roasted gram, packs of potato chips and pakoras, along with little tetra packs of frooti and small pouches of milk to be poured on the elephant's trunk. A few were even drawing designs with mehendi on the palms of women. Some were selling bottles of mineral water. Ojhai noticed that a few enterprising men had brought sturdy staffs to sell to those who might need the support of walking sticks in their climb. How they sold like hot cakes! They also passed by others who were already descending. Some stopped to pose for pictures. Birkhang hailed a young boy in multi-coloured sunglasses on his way down with a merry bobbing gait, unable to balance his body against gravity.

'Wahoi Jwhwlao!'

The boy waved back at the old man in true Bollywood style.

'Asidoh Buri…' Birkhang asked, '…is she still there? Still tells tales?'

The boy nodded. 'Already has a crowd listening to her,' he said without pausing.

As they walked up, every now and then Maikhoong would let out a sort of cheer-cry—'Jai Shiv Bwrai!'—to which his group and even others walking alongside would zealously respond: 'Jai!'

'Jai Baokhungri Hajw!' he would cheer a little later.

'Jai!' the people would cheer in response.

'Jai Bwisagu!'

'Jai!'

It was during that stretch of climbing without playing the siphoong that Ojhai and the rest passed by a young woman sitting on the felled trunk of an old sal tree. A young, anxious man stood by her, letting her lean her head on him while he gently patted her head with one hand. In the other hand, he held a bottle of water with its cap removed. Ojhai understood, she was drinking from it.

'They seem more than just lovers,' Ojhai said, turning to Birkhang and Daimalu.

'Need help, brother?' Gaorao shouted, sensing something wrong. For the young woman's lips looked white as a sheet. Gaorao stepped back from his team and walked towards the couple.

'All well?' he asked.

'Actually, Alaishri just fainted,' the young man standing with her replied.

'Oh!' was all Gaorao managed to say.

'But I need to reach Hatimatha,' the woman said feebly. 'I need to offer this milk,' she insisted, pointing towards the copper jar she was holding possessively, 'and bow at Shiv Bwrai's altar.' Her exhaustion was plainly visible.

'May we help?' Gaorao offered, though not understanding how they might be of any help at all. 'Oh, by the way, I am Gaorao.'

The man smiled. 'Iragdao,' he introduced himself, 'and my wife Alaishri.'

'Might she like to rest here if it's alright for you to carry the milk and offer it on her behalf?' Gaorao suggested.

Iragdao looked at Alaishri for an answer. Her face looked absolutely pale but she was adamant on going. 'I had promised Shiv Bwrai that I would come myself,' she protested.

'But it isn't wise. Not in your condition,' Iragdao tried to convince her.

Gaorao was in a fix. He didn't know what to say. So, instead, he spoke to the elderly woman a few feet away. She and her two young grandchildren were selling boiled eggs and nice, hot black tea. 'Hey, Madwi,' Gaorao addressed her, 'would you mind taking care of Alaishri till we return from Hatimatha?'

Gaorao looked at Iragdao for approval. He nodded in relief.

'For sure, young man,' said the elderly woman, tightening and tucking the dokhona over her chest as she offered Alaishri a styrofoam cup of steaming black tea.

'This will lighten your head and brighten those dimming eyes,' she said and felt Alaishri's forehead. 'Now trust this old Sonjila,' she said of herself. 'She has seen life and recognizes a woman with child when she sees one. So?' She winked at Iragdao. He blushed and smiled. Colour reappeared on Alaishri's cheeks and a glint reappeared in her eyes as she nodded coyly.

'Whoa!' Gaorao gasped. 'Then it makes greater sense for you to stay back and let Iragdao make the offering on your behalf.'

And so it was decided.

'Tell Shiv Bwrai, Irag, tell Him I was here last Bwisagu and the Bwisagu before that,' she said, sobbing. She was upset that destiny stopped her from visiting Bathou's altar for that third consecutive year. Iragdao and Gaorao had by then walked away, resuming their climb uphill.

'Tell Him I tried my best,' she cried after them.

Iragdao and Gaorao walked fast to catch up with Maikhoong and the rest.

'Well, you see,' Iragdao began to open up to Gaorao, 'after our first climb up these hills together, we got married. After the trek the next year, she conceived. She's with child now. And Alaishri feels it's all because of the blessings of Shiv Bwrai. That's why she was insistent on showing her gratitude this year. Well,' he paused for breath before resuming, 'she also fears that if she's unable to visit the altar for the third year at a stretch, something ominous will befall her. And us. And ours.'

'But hey, come on, it's all a belief,' Gaorao just about managed to say. 'Shiv Bwrai will understand.'

By then, the rest of the group had reached Hatimatha. A crowd of devotees thronged around Shiv Bwrai's modest altar, comprising a humble shivling under a mere tin-sheet roof and no side walls. The wide canopy of an old, large-girthed stone-apple tree sheltered it from the harshness of the wind and sun of the high hills. The priest inside was busy chanting prayers on behalf of a constant flow of believers since dawn. There was, however, a greater crowd flocking around Asidoh Buri. She sat a little distance away from the temple on a reed mat laid on the slightly raised circular base of the stone-apple tree. Chaitra's last sun was harsh that day, but what trickled in through the dense layers of thickly leafed boughs was just a wink of it, forming a trellis of light and shade on her fair face. No wonder fatigued trekkers found respite on the cool peak after an arduous climb. They loved to linger on even after paying their obeisance, before resuming their trek downhill. So, as the people lingered and walked around, soaking in the captivating view and getting a feel of the tales often told of olden times, they loved to sit around Asidoh Buri and hear from her the legend of Princess Diplai and the Baokhungri Hills. She kept no written record of events and read from none either. But when she narrated the lores, it seemed as if she had seen all of it unfold and occur before her very eyes. Only, the legends she spoke about were centuries old, which she wasn't. And yet, she never missed details.

Few realized she was an albino; most thought she was divine. It was the second thumb in both her hands that gave her the name Asidoh Buri. For the locals there, asi meant finger and doh was the number six. Of course, buri referred to old woman. Besides that, no one knew much about her. She always draped a dokhona without a blouse, be it summer or winter. And she narrated her tales mostly in Bodo. But sometimes, rarely, people heard her speak in fragmented Bangla too.

Ojhai, Daimalu and Birkhang had just come out of Shiv Bwrai's altar when Asidoh Buri called out, much to Ojhai's surprise.

'Nei, Ojhai! What is the siphoong for if you don't let your breath pass through it? Go on, enchant the abode of Bathou while I narrate tales of King Daukha and his bewitchingly charming daughter, Diplai Khungri.'

Ojhai smiled and brought out his siphoong as Asidoh Buri began her storytelling in her unique, sing-song manner. Her voice was as enthralling as the lores she sang about. Meanwhile,

Iragdao and Gaorao were still on their way to the peak but could hear Asidoh Buri's voice floating towards them.

'So, while the just King Daukha went hunting and fishing in the woods and waters of these forests, the lovely, lissom Diplai Khungri roamed around in these valleys, running and playing with her companions, singing with the birds and flitting with the butterflies. Sikhri, as they called them. And that's why, know all you who gather here, before even your grandmothers were born, Chakrashila was called Sikhri Sikhla—butterfly nymph. So now Diplai Khungri was the beloved and only daughter of the brave and benevolent King Daukha. Go down to the Bamwinijhora brook,' and she gestured with her fair, full arm stretched towards the valley, 'and you'll still see the canal made of stone, with five holes in it. Five,' she emphasized, raising her six fingers above her head. 'For five is an auspicious number for us Bodos. Five holes for fishing with the khokha.' She paused and searched out Ojhai in the crowd. 'Oi! Siphoong bwrai! Don't fall silent. Come, sit by me and play.'

Ojhai pushed ahead through the gathering and sat near her, facing Shiv Bwrai's temple. Iragdao and Gaorao had arrived by then and Ojhai saw them coming out of the temple. Iragdao walked towards the elephant's trunk to pour the milk on Alaishri's behalf. Ojhai's melody rang out through the Baokhungri Hills and through the dales and peaks all over Chakrashila, lending bounce to Asidoh Buri's voice as well.

'And so,' she resumed, 'on this last noon of Chaitra, hundreds of years ago, when the carefree princess bathed and basked under the spring sun, letting the Bwisagu breeze caress her supple limbs, news came to her that the love of her life lived no more. Alas! This prince of the neighbouring kingdom, valiant and handsome, whose thoughts kept the princess dreaming in her wakeful hours and awake in her dreams, whose love she held dearer than her own life, alas! Dear folks, news arrived that he had been killed in the ongoing war.' Asidoh Buri paused. Young girls sniffled into their dupattas; young men listened in awe. An ode rang out from Ojhai's siphoong in tribute to the love of the prince and the princess. The strains struck at the heartstrings of every lover there and even made the langurs halt mid-swing. A gentle breeze floated by, carrying the notes downhill to Alaishri.

Resting near Sonjila, Alaishri sat up with a start. 'That melody! That siphoong! I know it!' she exclaimed and suddenly stood up.

'Hey child! Slow! Slow!' Sonjila stood up after her. 'You don't just get up like sturdy me. What's wrong?'

Back at the Hatimatha peak, Asidoh Buri held her audience spellbound while heart-wrenching tunes from Ojhai's siphoong added melancholy to her narration. Despite the milling crowd around him, Ojhai felt the eerie sensation of an unseen presence about him once again.

Asidoh Buri continued: 'The shock and grief of the news bore down on the charming Princess Diplai like lightning. It hit her heart and shred it to pieces; it wrung her soul and left her insane. She did not know what more to live for. She did not know where else to look as she pined for her beloved.' The siphoong's pitch rose, but it was a sorrowful pitch.

'That pitch!' Alaishri said, looking up at the boughs above her. 'I know it! Yes, it is Abou Siphoong! I can't be mistaken. That kind of siphoong,' she said, gazing at Sonjila but stretching her hand towards the boughs, towards the flutenotes, 'only Abou makes them, for he plays no other. It is him. I must see him! I must go and meet him!' And she started to get up and walk up the hill. Sonjila hurried after her and grabbed her by the wrist, holding her back. 'No you can't, my dear,' she said with concern. 'Look at your condition.' But Alaishri was moving ahead, as if she hadn't heard Sonjila.

'You have to take care of the life breathing in you, Alaishri,' Sonjila kept repeating as she walked after her, still pulling her by the hand. 'Wait, Alaishri, don't get carried away now!' But Alaishri was oblivious to all else, except to the tunes from Ojhai's siphoong. Her steps almost fell into a run as she tried to pull her hand away from Sonjila.

'You know, Madwi,' Alaishri said as she kept walking ahead, pulling Sonjila after her, 'Abou Siphoong heard me play at a Bwisagu function many years ago when I was still a child. He so loved my rendition that he blessed me and gave me his own siphoong to hear me play it. He had said I could keep it if I so wished, if I promised to carry on playing the siphoong with a clear heart, with passion in it!'

'Oh! So you kept it?' Sonjila asked, suddenly finding it all very engaging and beginning to walk uphill with Alaishri. Alaishri looked down and shook her head sadly. 'The regret stayed with me,' she said. But as quickly, she was once again trying to pull herself away and run up the hill.

Asidoh Buri's narration was getting fast-paced now, carried away as she was by the grief of the princess. 'So, howling to the rocks and whimpering to the brooks,' she went on, 'no longer conscious of her deeds, she began running up these hills, these Baokhungri Hills, folks, the ones you climbed a while ago. Yes, these very hills, these same grounds she treaded, upon that you tread now.' Most in the gathering moved a few steps and looked down at the earth beneath their feet. 'Her beautiful long hair came undone and fell dishevelled all over her face and back. Her tears drained down her pink cheeks and thus she ran and ran, crying, beating her chest and calling her lover. Her companions and guards, they too ran after her. And like someone possessed, the princess kept running wildly up the hill.'

Alaishri was running up Baokhungri Hill. Ojhai's siphoong was drawing her to it and she followed its music.

The gathering in front of Asidoh Buri grew. But for sniffles and sighs, there was not a word or a noise that interrupted her storytelling. 'And when she reached the peak with nothing more left to climb and nothing more left to live for…' Ojhai's siphoong had reached such an intense blend of sorrow, pity and suspense that the rapt listeners forgot to breathe. A stone apple fell with a loud *thonk* upon the rusted tin shelter of Shiv Bwrai's temple. And yet, everyone remained unmoving, holding their breath.

'…The lovely, grieving Diplai Khungri…' Asidoh Buri took a deep breath and, as she released it, she sighed, 'killed herself!'

Somewhere downhill, Alaishri swooned. She had tried to steady herself but couldn't. Sonjila raised an alarm and those around helped carry her to the side of the foot track.

At the peak, sobs broke out. Ojhai's melody reached its climax, just as it reached Alaishri. But she did not hear it. For she had not yet regained her senses. Asidoh Buri paused, giving her listeners time to calm their sobs. And then she went on once more.

'From then on, this hill came to be known as Baokhungri. By "bao", the Bodos meant "renounce" and by "khungri", they meant princess. And so, as the princess renounced her life on these hills to join her love for all time to come, so it is believed that he who climbs this hill on this day is united with his love for the rest of his life on earth and thereafter too.'

The sobs ceased but the awe lingered. Someone rang the bell at Shiv Bwrai's altar. Asidoh Buri resumed her tale: 'The princess' maids and companions; remember they were following her?' The crowd nodded. 'Yes, faithful to their princess to the last, they followed her even in death. See those yonder hillocks?' she said, gesturing towards the valley. 'That is Mainao Bindw and over there, those are Bandra Hajw, Dangdufur and Najanggari. Just as Baokhungri Hill is named after Diplai Khungri, likewise, all those hillocks are named after one of her companions or the other. That one is Biliram Dakhri … Ah yes, over there, it is Khankhrikhola.' The people were slowly easing out towards the edge of the peak to take a look at the surrounding valleys, trying to locate the hillocks that Asidoh Buri was pointing towards. 'And they all have their own stories to tell, my dears, each of them! Each hillock!'

Downhill, Sonjila spread out a shawl on the ground. On it, she gently laid Alaishri. The women near her lent their jwmgras to roll and use as a pillow for Alaishri's head. One of them was fanning her head and another had to rub her feet, for they were turning cold.

Sonjila had earlier asked her grandchildren to mind the tea stall in her absence, but now she called out to them.

'Hurry, kids. Run up to Hatimatha and search him out. The man who came here with her. Will you recognize him?' The children nodded and immediately ran uphill.

'Now wait, you little typhoons,' Sonjila shouted after them. 'You'll need to know his name to ask around, you silly children! Say it's Iragdao! Understand? Ee-raag-dao!'

'Ou! Ou! Ou!' The children waved without turning back.

'Oh! Another thing!' Sonjila remembered and rushed after the children, shouting, 'Also ask for Maikhoong. And Abou Siphoong! Hear that? Oi!'

'Yes, yes!' they shouted back.

'Ojhai! Ojhai!' Sonjila shouted and waved. 'The siphoong player!'

But the children had already disappeared among the trekkers.

It didn't take much time for young, swift feet to reach the peak and for sharp youthful eyes to locate Iragdao. It was even easier for them to trace Ojhai, for they just followed the lilting notes of his siphoong.

'Alaishri has fainted,' the children panted and began to speak almost simultaneously to Iragdao but then took turns to convey the news.

Maikhoong, Iragdao and Gaorao immediately hurried down, while Rwngwra followed after gathering up his teammates and bringing them along with him.

Alaishri had come round by then, but she was clutching her stomach and cringing in excruciating pain, by turns clenching her teeth to hold back her cries and groans. When Iragdao came near, she clasped his hand and clung on. He felt his little world falling apart. He wouldn't be able to do without her and their yet unborn baby. He thought of the milk he had poured a while ago. He thought of Shiv Bwrai. But then his thoughts kept coming back to the woman in his arms. Alaishri. He loved her more than he loved Shiv Bwrai.

Maikhoong, Rwngwra and Gaorao had decided that they would take Alaishri and Iragdao with them in the Winger, and instead of going to their villages via Sijubagan, they would head straight to Kokrajhar town, to the Rupnath Brahma Civil Hospital.

They sat Alaishri on a plastic chair with arms, and a few men carried it to the foothill, where the Winger was parked. Iragdao walked beside her, holding her hand all through. Every now and then, Daimalu would tell the men bearing the chair: 'Careful, my boys!' or 'There, that's a rock over there, mind it, sons!' or 'Slow! Slow! She's wincing again!' And so Alaishri was carried down as gently as was possible.

Once they reached the vehicle, Iragdao carefully lifted her from the chair to the vehicle and made her lie down on the long seat at the rear end of the minibus with her head resting on his lap. One by one, the rest of the group began to arrive and board the bus. They were all quiet. Even if a few spoke, they did so in whispers, so as not to disturb Alaishri, and also because what they discussed was not meant for Alaishri and Iragdao to hear. For they were speaking among them about Alaishri and her baby. The baby, most were sure, was no more. Some even doubted Alaishri's ability to survive the upheavel. Nevertheless, they were all returning sombre. But Alaishri herself spoke aloud through her tears and pain.

'Abou Siphoong!' she said, looking at Iragdao. 'I had to meet him. I know he was there in the Baokhungri Hills. I heard his siphoong.' She didn't realize that he was in the same bus with her now. But Ojhai heard her. He turned to look at her and then slowly got up and walked towards her. 'I am Abou Siphoong,' he whispered softly, bending over her. 'It's me, child.'

The girl took her hands off her stomach and looked at the old man. Yes, it was that same face. As she stared at it unbelievingly, the flute notes she associated with that adorable face from long ago, from her childhood, echoed through her memory. She read those wrinkles which weren't there the last time she saw him. Her hand went back to her stomach. The child too wasn't there then. About now, she didn't know. She sobbed, bringing her palms together and raising her arms towards the old man. What surged through her was a mix of joy and sorrow. Joy, for having found Abou Siphoong when she was just beginning to think she had lost him once more. And sorrow, for she was beginning to think she was losing the child just when she had found motherhood.

'I am Alaishri,' she said. Her whole body shook in pain as she spoke, 'Remember me, Abou?'

Iragdao took it upon himself to bring to Ojhai's memory the day he had met a young Alaishri.

'You offered me your siphoong to play,' she said in between spasms of pain.

Ojhai's eyes lit up as it all came back to him—every moment of that delightful piece the girl had played as a child on his siphoong.

'But of course! Yes, I remember all of it now, yes!' he said, placing a hand on her head.

Alaishri broke down once again, writhing in intense agony and going back to clutching her stomach. 'Today, after I heard your siphoong, I just had to see you. I just had to meet you. Though I won't be able to play for you today, Abou, I'm sorry.' She choked.

Ojhai brought out the short siphoong from his bag and said, 'Never mind, today it shall be your Abou playing for you.'

And as the Winger rolled on to the highway towards Kokrajhar, Ojhai began playing his siphoong.

Pangs of guilt surged through his entire being as he began to play. Had it not been for her sincerety to meet him, Alaishri would not have ventured uphill in that condition, he thought. And then she would not have fainted and fallen. When Ojhai paused to breathe, he heard whispers towards the front of the minibus: 'It all looks so bleak'; 'I don't see the baby standing a chance'.

And each time he heard more of it, he felt as if a boulder fell on his heart, dragging it to the abyss of his guts.

*Am I responsible for it all?* he thought, remorse gnawing at his conscience. His siphoong could only dole out an apologetic lullaby as the Winger sped along the highway. There was no ecstatic rise and no dramatic fall of pitch. There was only a uniform, gentle flow of melody that spread all over the minibus, wrapping Alaishri and all other travellers in a caring embrace. That invisible embrace, amazingly, soothed Alaishri's cramped and excruciatingly painful abdomen. The muscles seemed to relax a bit. The wince upon her face gradually lifted, till it vanished completely. She felt a calm rising in her heart and encompassing her whole exhausted being as she let herself be taken over by the siphoong's strains. She had released her hold on her stomach and brought her hands to hold Iragdao's. The melody was lulling her to sleep.

'Please don't stop, Abou,' she said. Her words were slurred. Some in the minibus thought she was slipping out of consciousness again.

'May Shiv Bwrai keep at least one life breathing, if not both,' someone lamented in hushed tones. Ojhai's soul wilted and wept. Alaishri fell asleep, her head resting on Iragdao's lap, her hands still holding his.

When the Winger came to a halt at the Civil Hospital, Gaorao got off in a hurry and rushed in to arrange for a stretcher and talk to the doctor while Iragdao and a few others carefully brought Alaishri down. The stretcher arrived by then.

The sun was past its prime and ominous shadows began to prostrate along the wide corridors of the hospital, filling the heart with a greater sense of foreboding. As the men helped Alaishri on to the stretcher, Ojhai got off the minibus and walked towards it. He wanted to tell Alaishri how miserable he felt about the whole thing, that he wished to say sorry … but her eyes were closed. Putting up with all that pain had drained out all her energy. She was sleeping like a child with locks of her hair—wet with tears and sweat—clinging flaccidly to her pale face. Ojhai gently brushed them away. Assuming she was still unconscious, he stood next to the stretcher, not saying anything of everything that he hoped to tell her before she went in. Every breath he took filled his heart with more guilt. He quietly took out the small siphoong from his bag and softly slid it under her pillow.

'May she play it for her child when she has one. Someday.' He prayed silently.

Iragdao put a hand on the old man's arm and nodded, as if thanking him on Alaishri's behalf. Ojhai's eyes welled up and tears trickled down his wrinkled face. He bent to kiss her head, but the stretcher was already being wheeled away, leading to a few drops of tears to fall on her stomach instead. He watched till the stretcher turned at the far corner of the corridor and disappeared from sight before walking back to the minibus. Gaorao stayed back with Iragdao at the hospital while the bus left with the rest of the passengers.

On the way back, Ojhai, Daimalu and Birkhang didn't speak a word. They couldn't. Daimalu and Birkhang heard Ojhai sobbing. They didn't stop him.

It was Bwisagu the next day. But there was no spring in Ojhai's heart, no festivity at all. He didn't even come out of the house. It was only when Daimalu and Birkhang arrived later in the day that they coaxed him out into the courtyard for a while. However, for the first time ever, they saw Ojhai without his siphoong, that too during Bwisagu. Even in the months that followed, Ojhai never played it again, except during prayers at the Bathou temple. Laughter, cheer and music had lifted from his once-carefree life. In their place, remorse sat heavy. Every morning he woke up cursing himself for having brought this suffering upon Alaishri.

'But Shiv Bwrai,' Ojhai often wondered, staring at the Sijou plant in his courtyard, 'why did you let it happen when I placed all my trust in you?'

Spring and summer thus passed by that year with Ojhai withdrawing into himself. His siphoong sat passively in a corner of his room among other things. Then, one lazy afternoon, towards mid-autumn, Ojhai's daughter-in-law came running to him and announced, 'Apha! Apha! There's someone in the courtyard to meet you!' She sounded absolutely delighted.

'Who?' He asked, with no eagerness whatsoever.

'Don't know, never seen them before. A couple,' she said, unable to withhold her joy.

With slow, uninterested steps, Ojhai walked out into the courtyard. There, sitting on a bench, were Alaishri and Iragdao, each holding a tiny bundle.

'Twins, Abou!' Alaishri squealed excitedly the moment she saw Ojhai.

Ojhai's steps froze and he was rendered speechless. It took some time for him to grasp the sudden developments—the news that was related to the guilt that had been sitting heavy on his soul all these months. The next instant, he was running towards them to fold all four of them in his arms. All of a sudden, his heart felt light as the whistle of his siphoong and laughter rose from its depths. But when he held the four in his embrace, he cried instead like a baby, perhaps to wash away every speckle of guilt that sat like stains on his conscience all this while.

'The babies have arrived, Abou!' Iragdao spoke at last. 'Later that evening at the hospital, the doctor herself was amazed when the test reports came. She said it was nothing short of a miracle. You know what she said, Abou?'

'She said what?' Ojhai asked, bent over the babies.

'She said that something deeply comforting helped the foetuses to overcome the trauma of the shock caused by the fall,' Iragdao explained. 'And the fall had every possibility of the worst kind of consequences…'

Ojhai nodded. No one understood those consequences better than him.

Iragdao went on: 'She said some extraordinary thing must have soothed and lulled the babies to sleep and that sleep, it seemed, worked as a pain killer. As an anaesthetic. It seemed something almost divine and very passionate took care of the foetuses in those extremely crucial hours between the moment of shock and the commencement of medical treatment.'

Ojhai was still looking at the babies, tickling their toes and smelling their heads. He was beside himself with joy.

'The doctor asked us, Abou, what could have been that intervening factor. Whether it was some specific smell, or someone's touch or maybe some kind of music...'

Ojhai looked up and smiled, 'She asked thus?'

'She did, Abou,' Alaishri pitched in. 'We owe our babies to you. That's why we have brought them here to seek your blessings ... And also, Abou,' she gulped, 'we wish for you to please name them.'

'This is a girl here,' Iragdao said, smiling at the baby in his arms. 'And there, with Alaishri, that's a boy!'

With the lightness of a guilt-free heart and a voice that quivered from sheer thrill, Ojhai blurted out without even stopping for an instant to think and decide: 'The little girl, let me call her Serja. And there, my boy, you are Siphoong!'

***

Ojhai, Daimalu and Birkhang boarded the bus to Chakrashila about a fortnight later to revisit Shiv Bwrai's temple at Hatimatha. Ojhai wished to offer his gratitude to Bathou for saving Alaishri's babies and for lifting from his heart the burden of guilt. The hill was quiet and serene that morning, almost mysterious in its allure. There wasn't another human in sight as the friends climbed up. Fallen leaves of autumn rustled under their feet and langurs screeched above their heads. Large flocks of hill birds took off in alarm when they heard people approaching. After paying their obeisance at Shiv Bwrai's altar, Ojhai hesitantly took out his siphoong and played it. And it amazed him, for he no longer felt the uncanny presence of someone lurking around. He played long and he played varying tunes at leisure, as if to convince himself. By the end of it, he was assured of the invisible presence having been liberated from the Baokhungri Hills, just as his heart was after the guilt lifted from it. He played some more, and all he felt was a deep calm that swept through every pore of his old body.

That day, as they climbed down, the Baokhungri Hill put back all the laughter, cheer and music back into Ojhai's life, making it carefree once more!

# Chapter 8

# ESCAPE

Ojhai no longer remembered the year.

But the scanty hair on his arms still rose, and little beads of sweat still appeared on the tip of his small nose when those faraway, cold cries of a mob seeking vengeance and rebellion shrieked through memory to reach his ears, like that false dawn of many years ago, during the times of the agitation for statehood.

***

'Damn! Damn! Those reckless fools! Jamba fwr!'

Breathless, and his shirt sticking to his sweaty back, Daimalu had kept looking over his shoulders that dawn as he came almost running through the fields and wilderness, avoiding the usual path to their village. He was scared that the army might be at his heels. Ojhai's house came well before his from that end of the village; so it was there that he rushed in. He was fleeing, terrified that he might be leading the army personnel into their village. 'Those fools!' he panted. 'They have burnt down the Dholamari Bridge!'

The last of the night birds had not yet reached their homes, and the pale-grey leftovers of a sultry June night were yet to be swept off the sky. Alarmed, Ojhai hurried out into the courtyard, hearing Daimalu's voice so early in the day. They all knew what the Dholamari incident on National Highway 31 would lead to. And yet, panic seemed to have pushed the words out of Ojhai: 'What now?'

'What else,' Daimalu sat down, wiping the sweat off his brow with his aronai. 'Those armymen will stomp down our villages looking for the boys.'

'Hush, Daimalu, hush!' Ojhai tried to calm him even as he heard his own heart's rising unrest.

'Are all our young boys safely out of the village?' Daimalu asked when he got his breath back.

Ojhai thought for a while, trying to recollect. By now, the warbles and sharp chirps of the early-morning birds were slowly beginning to fill the silence and, from afar, the faint clanging of the previous night's unwashed pots and pans being carried to the well began to float in. Those were the times when the elderly, the womenfolk and the children shut themselves in long before sundown out of fear of the security forces and the rebels. Some of the young boys had long fled their homes and villages, lest they be taken away forcefully to the training camps of the extremists, or picked up randomly by the police for questioning; but most were already away at the camps in the hills and forests, training to shoot homemade firearms and to throw handmade grenades. Bloodshed and turmoil had come to stay in the Bodo areas since the demand for a separate state had gone on to become a full-blown uprising. 'Only as a consequence of the deprivation and prejudice that tribal people were made to endure since the ancient times,' they claimed.

And then the rebels had burnt down a bridge, which would disrupt essential movement in a major route. Ojhai found his voice at last: 'Our boys … yes, they should all be out safe,' he replied thoughtfully. 'But why the Dholamari Bridge?'

'Aah, come now, Ojhai, every bridge, every government office is a target, you know very well. Why ask?' Daimalu stood up and stretched his back. 'The police had picked up three boys from Phakribeel about a fortnight ago, remember?'

Ojhai nodded. 'I do. One of them was Birkhang's young nephew. Bonjoi.' Ojhai paused before wondering aloud: 'Wasn't Thompson his elder brother? The one who had long fled the village like most boys his age?'

'Hmm,' Daimalu replied, 'but Bonjoi was only sixteen. Who would have thought such a small boy would be dragged away by the police?'

The bullet-ridden bodies of those three boys from Phakribeel were found a few days later in the marshes beyond Birkhang's paddy fields. The newspapers had screamed, *killed in an encounter while escaping from police custody*.

'Lies! Lies, all of it!' Bonjoi's father had cried hysterically, repeatedly striking his dao against the trunk of the betel nut tree at the edge of their courtyard. 'Murderers! They killed my little boy! They shot him just because he couldn't tell them about his brother Thompson! Killers!'

Bonjoi's mother Romola was in the kitchen by the fire, preparing the evening meal when they brought home his muddied, blood-smeared and disfigured body wrapped in an old, torn tarpaulin hanging from a bamboo pole; like slaughtered pig. As she stood up with a start, the ladle dropped from her hand and her mouth opened wide, but no sound escaped it. Her face twitched, her eyes rolled back and she collapsed upon the ground, clutching her chest. Her trembling feet struck down the saucepan of boiling rice from the fire and the steaming contents poured out all over her legs. Smothered in the piping hot rice and still bubbling water, her feet were beginning to scald. Flints of fire from the hearth began to feed along the edge of her dokhona. But the poor woman did not feel any of this ordeal, for she had already become unconscious from a massive stroke.

Romola survived the stroke, but not that she knew of it. For she had ceased to know or feel anything at all since that moment in the kitchen. She had only been breathing and staring right through the rafters of their thatched roof, without seeing anything, her limbs lying dead next to her wasting body.

As Ojhai waited in his yard with Daimalu, a heavy silence hung between them till a large flight of crows flew overhead, shredding the silence with their impetuous cawing. The men looked up. The crows were flying away from the direction of the raging bridge, driven away by the thick swirls of dark smoke that rose into the morning sky like a sinister tornado. The air began to reek of a concoction of burnt metal, rubber and explosives.

'The Dholamari Bridge is an answer to that fake encounter, Ojhai. Has Birkhang been told about the bridge?' Daimalu asked, suddenly anxious.

On an impulse, both men turned and started walking towards Birkhang's house, to inform him. Ojhai instinctively reached into the tuck of the phali at his waist, to feel for his siphoong. It was there. For Ojhai never stepped out of his room without it. The siphoong was his soul. And now, as he let his fingers tighten around it, it drove through him a sense of reassurance and courage. Though the morning sun shone down on the fields and though it was time to ready the fields for sowing, there was no one ploughing them and the fields lay achingly desolate.

'This season too there will be no harvest,' Ojhai sighed.

They quickened their pace and walked past the Madlagami L.P. School. At an hour when little children ought to have been filling into their classes, when laughter and prattle ought to have livened the school's classrooms, they remained deafeningly silent and deserted, except for the stray creaking of a windowpane jostled by breeze every now and then. Thojen's cows were grazing on the overgrown grass of the school's large yard; overgrown because little feet long stopped walking and playing on them. Schools and colleges had come to a virtual close. No one knew when they would reopen. Some had even been turned into relief camps.

The men's steps fell faster and faster as sirens of fire trucks, rushing towards the bridge, wailed through the village. The few people who had come out with their cattle, hurried back home. Ojhai and Daimalu almost fell into a run till they reached Birkhang's house.

That morning, they did not start calling him from the courtyard itself, as they usually did. They instead rushed to the western hutment of Birkhang's homestead and began thumping furiously at the door of his room, all the while turning back to see if someone had caught up with them, someone who ought not to. While the men almost thrust their noses at the door, Birkhang appeared from behind the coconut-palm fence around the well, from the other side of the courtyard.

'The Dholamari Bridge, eh?' Birkhang said from behind. His voice startled the already edgy Ojhai and Daimalu. 'Mergau just ran in, informed us and ran out,' Birkhang said, wiping his face with a gamosa.

'All clear?' Ojhai asked, swift and short.

Birkhang nodded.

Daimalu still looked pale, despite the radiant sun now shining down on them in the courtyard. 'So now when those armymen and police will not be able to lay hands on our boys, they will ransack our granaries and rape our women to make us talk about the hideout of our boys. Their rifle butts will crack our skulls. And when the boys get to know of this, they will resort to more violence, more protests ... Have you realized something? There are hardly any more bridges left to be destroyed. State or no State, I just wish for this violence to end. Whoever may benefit out of this, my friends, it is certainly not the common village folk like you and me. At this age, I've seen enough. I just wish for peace now.'

***

In a small, inconspicuous tea stall within the campus of the Gauhati Medical College and Hospital, Thompson had been working as an errand boy for quite some time now, as much to earn a livelihood as to remain in hiding. News of Bonjoi's death had reached him; yet, he could not go to see the last of his little brother. Trains through that region had stopped running and more than hundred hours of bandh at a stretch in the Bodoland Territorial Area District had brought all public transport to a crippling halt. The afternoon the news reached him, Thompson cried bitterly into the nook of his tanned, lean arms, crouching in a corner outside the tea stall. The clatter of cups and plates and the drone of conversation among customers drowned the grief that lacerated his heart. How it yearned to go home, to be with his folks, to see his little brother for one last time! He wanted to run away and reach home, whatever be the cost. But the owner of the tea stall had stopped him.

'Look, Thompson,' he had said, 'I feel for you and I understand your pain. But how will you reach home without falling into the hands of the security forces? It's everywhere—the TV, the newspapers and even people's conversations, that your place is teeming with the armed forces, looking out for insurgents and boys like you. What if they get you? Don't you think your parents need you? Now that…' he trailed off, seeing Thompson's eyes reddening and brimming over. And so Thompson stayed back, tossing and turning through the nights, hoping that someone from home would soon be at the hospital with news from home.

The tea stall suited him, because whenever people from around his village came to the hospital, which they did whenever protests and bandhs did not disrupt vehicular movement, Thompson got news from home. This was the only thing that kept him going. It wasn't really difficult for him to find folks from home. He would saunter into the corridors of the many wards inside the hospital, carrying a stack of disposable paper cups in one hand, a packet of assorted cakes and biscuits in the other, and a flask of steaming tea hanging from a belt slung across his shoulder. There was never a dearth of people wanting some tea. And as he went about vending tea, he looked out for women in the dokhona and men in the phali. This was how, just last week, he had come upon his Aunt Gaojeng and her husband who were at the hospital to remove a tumor from Aunt Gaojeng's uterus.

'But, Thompson, it would be good, son, if you could manage to visit home once. It would do good to Romola. She is wasting away and may not wait too long,' Gaojeng had said.

Thompson listened quietly, pouring out the cups of tea absent mindedly, but with an ease that came from routinely doing a task a hundred times a day. He then handed them out to his aunt and uncle and held out the packet of assorted cakes and biscuits to them so that they could have their pick. Standing outside the Female Surgical Ward, he looked around to see if anyone else wanted his offerings.

'When is the surgery, Madwi?' he asked his aunt.

'The surgery is done. We'll leave in a couple of days. We are just waiting for a safe day. It seems some arrangement has been made for ambulances and a few other vehicles to go together,' his uncle said. 'If necessary, I heard them say, they may even provide police escort.'

Thompson stood by listening to more stories from home as Gaojeng and her husband drank their tea. When they finished, he took the cups from them, walked over to the bin and dropped them into it, as if the activity were part of his tea vending.

'I'll come back later today, Madwi,' he said as he walked away through the corridors, down the ramp for stretchers and wheelchairs, lost in thought. He had always felt nauseated with the smell of medicine, disinfectants and stale food around those corridors and passages, but today he was beyond registering any of it. His mind was thinking hard: of possible ways to get into the ambulance with his aunt and uncle. Maybe as an attendant. Gaojeng's parting words that day—'she may not wait too long'—kept assaulting his heart all through that night and the days that followed. He would go away, go home, to see his mother before it was too late.

A day later, Gaojeng, her husband and Thompson were sitting in a private ambulance along with two others to reach home in the Bodoland Territorial Area District. An elderly man lay on a stretcher, with tell-tale tapes across his wrists and the insides of his elbows, covering cannula insertion bruises. Anxiety was writ large upon each of their faces.

'No road blockades today, are you sure?' someone asked the driver.

'Not that I have been told of,' he responded glumly. 'Though in some stretches of the highway, there just might be protests by local agitators. There always is something. If so, we might see car tyres burning in the middle of the road and possibly some stonepelting. Just letting you know.' He paused. The man lying on the stretcher was visibly in trauma. He was being shifted to the Bongaigaon Civil Hospital. The driver went on, 'There is usually a police escort for ambulances. But then who knows what goes on in the minds of those rebelling against the government machinery and the police?' He didn't speak another word during the entire journey till they reached Bongaigaon. From there, Thompson's aunt and uncle took an auto-rickshaw to their home in Barhiguri. Thompson accompanied them but got off just before the auto-rickshaw arrived in Barhiguri. Then, abandoning the highway, he stepped into the vast expanse of tall, wild grass that rolled out from the highway till the small river that flowed right past the field in their backyard. The sharp edges of the grass cut his face and bruised his arms and feet as he waded through them. Each time he parted the grass to make way, he prayed fervently that the movement of the grass above his head would go unnoticed. On many occasions in the past, he had walked his way through that scuffling undergrowth. But those times were different. He was not alone then and he had friends fleeing with him. His mother too was well then ... and Bonjoi was home. Pushing his way alone through the insect-ridden grass now, sometimes running and sometimes crawling, he emerged on the banks of the river. His breath was getting faster and shorter, his legs beginning to wobble. He took a deep, long breath and plunged into the waters, shirt and all, and began swimming under water for as long as he could hold his breath. Every now and then, he raised his head above the waters for short spurts, gulped in more air and dived back in and continued to swim till he reached the far end of the river, just behind his home. Fatigue had so immensely overpowered his limbs that he could barely pull himself out of the waters.

When he eventually managed to drag himself ashore, he could see glimpses of the thatch roof of their house in the distance, through the betel nut trees. Home! Mother! He was almost there, but too exhausted to get up and start walking. He fell upon the ground and just lay there, the hard clods of earth hurting his wet back. His eyelids fell together, and he thought he heard the faint echo of familiar, endearing whistles of a siphoong floating towards him. How those strains soothed his bruised body and tormented mind! They helped Thompson regain the strength in his legs; home was now just a few paces away.

By dusk that day, villagers heard the roar of a vehicle rumbling through the dry, bumpy mud roads of the village. Soon, Ojhai heard the familiar stomp of army boots walking into their homestead and surrounding the hutments. They were in Ojhai's courtyard.

Ojhai had just put his fingers into a plate of comforting, steaming rice, about to have his supper. He got up from his khamplai and peeked out of the kitchen through a crack in the old, wooden windowpane.

'They're here,' he whispered to his son and daughter-in-law.

'They must have got information about Thompson,' his son said, in hushed tones.

'What information?' Ojhai asked.

'Why, Thompson is home, Apha. Looks like Madwi Romola won't make it through the night,' Ojhai's son said.

'Dear Lord! They won't spare that boy if they get their hands on him.'

Ojhai's daughter-in-law reduced the flame of the wicker lamp. The silhouettes stomping about in the yard terrified her, but such intrusions were regular during the times of the agitation.

'Anyone in there? Come out, please!' One of the armymen was stepping closer to the kitchen. Ojhai walked towards the door.

'No! Apha!' His son caught him by the wrist and pulled him back.

Ojhai's daughter-in-law tapped her husband on the shoulder from behind and, when he turned around, she said softly under her breath, 'Let him. He knows what he is doing.' She placed all her trust in Ojhai and the old man never failed her.

'Stay where you are,' Ojhai told his children as he opened the door and walked out of the kitchen. Then, gently closing the door behind him, he stepped out into the courtyard, alone into the midst of the armed men. He was uncertain of what lay ahead, but he had a purpose. A noble one.

'You aren't alone, are you?' the armyman asked him. Two more walked towards the back of the kitchen.

'No, I am not,' Ojhai replied, showing the least sign of nervousness.

'Who else, then? In there?'

'Why, my old woman.'

'That's all?'

'Aah, if you take a little child into consideration, he's there with her.'

The sky had now turned a deep, blackish blue and darkness took over every corner of the yard.

'We have information that a young man has arrived in the village this afternoon.'

Ojhai felt grateful for the darkness, for they could not read his face.

The two men who had gone towards the back had now come up to Ojhai and one was walking towards the kitchen, the bayonet of his weapon pointing towards the kitchen door. Ojhai felt for the siphoong at his waist. That was his weapon—his strength and his amulet against all peril. He derived his courage from it. Just as the man was about to step onto the raised verandah of the kitchen, Ojhai quickly turned towards him and said, 'But you will incur the wrath of a grandmother trying desperately to lull her little grandson to sleep.'

Behind the closed doors of the kitchen, Ojhai's daughter-in-law began to hum a lullaby just loud enough for the sound to reach out till the raised verandah.

Oi okhapwr, fwi, fwi!
Nwngfwiyaabwla thaler thaiseh hor,
Thaler thaiseh horaa bwla thaler thaineh hor
Fwi fwi oi okhapwr!

*O Moon! Come, come!*
*If you won't, then give me a banana,*
*If not one, then make it two!*
*Come, come O moon!*

The man paused.

Ojhai continued: 'The child doesn't sleep till I play my siphoong and the old woman sings to him.' Saying so, he pulled out the siphoong from his waist and took it to his lips. Playing by instinct and hoping against hope, Ojhai whistled into his siphoong and let the magic wand do the rest. Soon, the notes began to cascade gently into the night, gradually making the armymen ease away from their alert positions, let down their guard and hold down their weapons. The men listened to the siphoong, bliss seeping into their souls. Just a few moments of that bliss would neither harm nor make a difference to their search, they thought. As it was, the night seemed to be an uneventful one in the village, for everything lay calm and silent. One man sat down on the verandah. Ojhai felt encouraged and played on. Then, bringing his siphoong down, he sang in the same soft, lulling melody, hoping with all his heart that the men didn't understand Bodo.

*Into the night, my son,*
*Go stealthily and alone,*
*Make good the escape of the dying woman's own.*
*Ask of them not to moan,*
*Life is just a sojourn,*
*Go stealthily and alone,*
*Make good the escape of the dying woman's own.*

Ojhai then played the melody on his siphoong and sang the verse again, a little louder this time.

Inside the dimly lit, mud-floored kitchen, Ojhai's son turned to his wife. She nodded, tiptoed to the hearth and caused little distracting noises, tinkering with the firewood, the pan and random utensils, allowing her husband to quietly unlatch the lone window on the back wall, climb out and disappear into the night along the covert trail that the cat took to the kitchen. And Ojhai played on, gently beginning to sway to his own melody, drawing the mysterious enchantment of the night into the yard.

As the notes began to get more and more passionate and sailed out through the growing darkness to reach Daimalu and Birkhang, they knew Ojhai needed them. For it wasn't usual of Ojhai and his siphoong to dole out their soulful strains during that hour of the spirits. That too when they all heard an army vehicle rumble into the village earlier in the evening. So they both came out and started for Ojhai's house, Birkhang hanging his kham across his shoulder and Daimalu with his jotha in his hands. And to quell the many fears caused by the night, the apprehension of the moment and the army vehicle, Birkhang began to lightly beat his kham and Daimalu began to clap his jotha as they walked briskly but without speaking a word. That night, the otherwise comforting chirp of the crickets and cicadas only sent shivers down their backs. As they got closer to Ojhai's yard, their beats began to fall in rhythm with Ojhai's notes. How it rejuvenated Ojhai's falling hopes! When Ojhai noticed the armymen looking alarmed, he explained: 'Not to worry, these are just friends—old men like me. Do you think there are any young men left in the village to walk into your way?' He let the corners of his mouth droop and shook his head, in response to his own question.

Ojhai then pointed towards the kitchen and began to tell the armymen: 'You see, they both are similar, women and the siphoong. They both can amazingly play as many notes as even the Gods have not yet created!' One more armyman went and sat on the raised verandah of the northern hutment, in front of the door to Ojhai's room. Another leaned against a wooden post next to him. Ojhai shifted from broken Hindi to hand gestures, to facial expressions, and then to a rise and fall of pitch as he spoke to the men, making every effort to make them understand his narrative, and at the same time, to veil the turbulence in his heart. 'She can be a grandmother,' he pointed once more with his siphoong towards the kitchen, 'one that sings the gentlest of lullabies, or one that rolls her eyes and spews fire to discipline.' Ojhai raised the siphoong to his lips and played a tune so soft and lilting that he was sure he heard one of the men sniffle. 'That,' he explained, 'is the grandmother singing a lullaby.' Then he quickly shifted to a fast, pulsating tune, for the chastising grandmother. 'Then there is the younger sister, who persuades her elder brother to bring her a pair of silver earrings when he comes home on leave.' The siphoong's notes now rose and fell, sometimes in brisk little waves and sometimes in long, low and persuading tones, as if demanding and beseeching at the same time—like the brisk prancing and long sulk of a little sister. One from the armymen propped his weapon between his legs and, digging into an inner pocket of his thick uniform, pulled out a brown envelope, folded twice over. He unfolded it as he walked towards Ojhai and pulled out what turned out to be a family photograph. 'This,' he said, holding the picture up for some moonlight to shine on it, and pointing at a young girl with two ribboned braids falling on either side of her chest, and a pretty smile, 'is my sister. Payal. She is getting married next week and I had promised her a pair of earrings as a gift.' His voice choked. 'I didn't get leave to go home.'

Slowly, the siphoong's notes began to seep deeper into the hearts of the armymen and stirred their souls. Birkhang and Daimalu glided into the courtyard, even as nervousness rose from their guts and flooded their hearts. Walking into a courtyard full of armymen at a time when they held villages in the grip of terror was no old man's song and dance. Even the uniformed men looked at Birkhang and Daimalu with some suspicion. But artful that Ojhai was, he convinced both sides and the impromptu concert resumed. Alone inside the kitchen, his daughter-in-law grew more and more restless, as memories and stories of police atrocities and army–insurgent clashes began to haunt her in the darkness. Each time she stopped hearing the siphoong, her heart too stopped, beating again only when the siphoong's notes soared.

'Now the little daughter,' Ojhai said and began to play a merry, bouncing tune, cheer emanating from every tap of his deft, stout fingers in the little holes of the flute. It was a happy chaos of rhapsody and distune, like the prattle of a child that never went by rule and form, yet that was what made it delightful. A smile spread across the face of one of the armymen. In the faint starlight, Ojhai saw the twinkle in his eyes as he spoke to the man standing next to him: 'That's like my daughter. She spoke to me a couple of days ago through a neighbour's phone.' Then he turned to Birkhang and said, 'Her mother said she has started going to school. And she sang a nursery rhyme for me, which was amusingly out of tune, just like the notes of the flute.'

Ojhai's heart melted.

He took a breather and swung around with his arms in the air, holding his siphoong high. 'Hoi! Hoi!' he said cheerfully. 'And then there is the lover, the consort, the wife, the mistress! She is passion! She is strength, she is weakness! As is the flute!' And saying so, he let the siphoong caress his cheek and lips before he began to whistle into it. This time, he crooned lustily, letting each note of the siphoong fondle every inch of the men's muscled, taut but lovelorn bodies and starving souls, allowing the passion to grow little by little till it consumed their screaming, wrung-out beings. Like the first spells of monsoon upon the parched, cracked earth, the spells of the siphoong quenched the thirst of the men's parched emotions, its charm completely binding the armymen into a trance. Clapping his jotha with incredible skill of his agile wrists, Daimalu sauntered closer to one of the more vulnerable men and danced around him as he would around a lady during Bwisagu. Little waves of laughter arose from the rest. And the melody turned so tormenting and lovesick that the men's hearts began to ache. They began to pine for their wives and their betrothed. One clutched his heart and turning his back to the group, looked up and kept staring at the stars in the sky. A few began to dance.

Ojhai too looked up at the sky. The night had moved into a deep dark, the stars were many now. Drumming at the sides of his kham, Birkhang tapped his feet in rhythm with his hands. Moving as he did so, he danced towards the centre of the courtyard, then to the northern edge, and back to the centre and again to the eastern edge, all the while beating his drum and sensing for movements around the yard and towards the back of the kitchen. Daimalu picked the cue and filled in the gaps left by the beats with the claps of his jotha. No one noticed that taking cover of the distraction, the window at the back of the kitchen wall once more got opened very quietly and shut back as noiselessly and swiftly. Birkhang began to beat the kham more vigorously and looking at Ojhai, nodded his head from side to side with great gusto.

'Then there is the woman who is a mother,' Ojhai went on, 'understanding, sacrificing, keeping her pain to herself and bearing that of her children's as well.' He tucked his siphoong back into the phali, walked into his room and brought out a different, longer one. 'The mother is always just so much more than the rest, you see,' and looking down at the siphoong in his hand, said, 'and is always special.' He touched his forehead with it before taking it to his lips.

The notes serenaded into the night, rising gradually, now compelling and now surrendering as they calmed the disturbed heart and steadied the reckless mind. They picked at chords buried in the deepest recesses of the armymen's hearts, taking them back into a childhood of happy times when they walked with their mothers to village fairs and festivals. One of the men remembered how his mother had bought him a flute in one of the fairs by the Yamuna river. He raised his arms and began to move them in sync with Ojhai's tunes, nodding his head. Seeing this, Birkhang quickened the pace of his drumbeat and Daimalu let his jotha go with it. Gentle yet powerful, the siphoong's melody embraced the men with a strange feeling of comfort and peace, despite the fear lurking in the night between the two sets of men. Letting the tune reach a crescendo, Ojhai stopped suddenly. 'Then one fine day,' he narrated, 'just when we begin taking our mothers for granted,' he paused and took a deep breath, 'they leave for the other world.'

The mood in the courtyard turned sombre.

The army men whose mother bought him a flute came close to Ojhai and hesitantly, almost begged, 'May I try the siphoong, please?'

Birkhang's jaw dropped, he looked at Daimalu. Silence and apprehension engulfed the yard. He who wielded a gun was now imploring for the flute.

'Will he shoot if Ojhai refuses?' Daimalu was petrified.

*Might they run amok through the village, bringing in more of their tribe and cause a carnage?* Birkhang panicked.

But Ojhai was calm as ever.

'And why not?' he said, stretching out his hand with the flute to the armyman. The rest looked on, stupefied. The siphoong could as well have been a twig of olive. 'Please, go on. Nothing would bring me more joy at a time like this.'

The man took the siphoong in both hands with immense reverence and, just as he was about to play it, wails and shrieks pierced through the night and ripped it apart.

'Quick!' One of the men jumped up, steadied his weapon and commanded the rest to raise their guards, which they had let down for quite some time now. 'Move!' he shouted. 'Move! Move!'

The three old friends looked at one another. The wails floated in from the direction of Romola's house.

'She's gone!' Daimalu uttered under his breath.

'The boy?' Ojhai's eyes asked.

Birkhang blinked very slowly.

The armymen began to hurry out of Ojhai's yard and, instead of taking the clear but winding, narrow foot track towards Romola's yard, they cut short through the betel nut grove. The man who had borrowed the siphoong stepped back towards Ojhai and handed it back to him, but Ojhai gently pushed away the man's hand. It felt coarse and sinewy.

'Take it with you, my friend,' Ojhai said, 'as a memory of a few cherished moments of a fateful night. Whistle into it whenever your heart feels lonely. I shall hear your melody and let mine reach out to yours. Go now, dear friend, duty calls!'

The man clasped Ojhai's hand with his, nodded at Birkhang and Daimalu, and sped away to catch up with the rest. As he walked, he tucked the siphoong into the thick army belt around his lean waist, just the way Ojhai did his siphoong into the aronai on his waist.

When the stomp of army boots receded into the night, Ojhai's daughter-in-law raised the wick of the lantern inside the kitchen.

Meanwhile, past the large expanse of tall grass, inside a moss-layered, leech-infested narrow culvert farther down the small river, Thompson lay curled into himself like a fetus. It was wet and cold in there. He shivered. His legs would carry him no further—not for now. He lay there hugging his knees tight, just the way he had hugged his mother during her last few breaths, too scared even to cry, lest someone heard. And now as he lay limp and bruised, the river gently washed his sores as it flowed past him under the culvert and to Thompson's ears, the murmur of the flowing waters felt soothing like the croon from Ojhai's siphoong.

Thompson had escaped.

# GLOSSARY OF BODO TERMS

Abou: Grandfather

Aronai: Narrow stole used by Bodo men

Ayei: Endearing term for mother

Bathou: Shiva

Bagurumba: Folk dance of the Bodos

Bwisagu: Bodo new year and spring festival

Bwrai: Old person; oldest or most senior in power and knowledge

Dao: Single-edged broadsword

Dhaal: Shield

Dokhona: Traditional costume of Bodo women

Gamosa: A piece of cloth the length of a stole, used to felicitate someone; also used as a towel

Gwkha-gwkhei: Bitter-sour

Habab!: Common Bodo exclamatory term

Hajwgakhwnai: Hill climbing

Ingkhri: Curry

Jamba fwr: Fools

Janwsei lwngnwsei: Eat and drink

Japkhring: Musical instrument consisting of metallic discs in a wooden frame

Jekhai/khobai/pholo/khokha: Fishing equipments made using cane or bamboo

Jou/joubidei: Fermented rice beer

Jwhwlao: Hero

Jwmgra: Women's stole

Kham: Long drum

Khamplai: Low, rectangular wooden stool to sit on

Kharei: Alkali or soda

Labra: A dish made with assorted vegetables

Laru, sithau: Snacks made of rice powder

Madwi: Aunt

Mekhela: Lower half of a two-piece women's garment

Mwiderkhafal: Elephant's forehead

Nwngou: Yes

Oja: Priest

Oma khasi: Neutered pig

Ondla: Rice flour

Phali: Traditional knee-length garment of Bodo men, wrapped around the waist

Phithikhri: A variety of small fish

Sengra: Youth
Serja: A four-stringed musical instrument
Sijou: Euphorbia plant
Siphoong: Flute

Thungri: Long battle sword